A Haunting at Hollow's Cove

Jeff DeGordick

Copyright © 2018 by Jeff DeGordick

All rights reserved. No part of this publication may be reproduced or transmitted in any form or by any means, electronic, mechanical or otherwise, without written permission from the author.

This is a work of fiction. Names, characters, businesses, places, events and incidents are either the products of the author's imagination or used in a fictitious manner. Any resemblance to actual persons, living or dead, or actual events is purely coincidental.

Cover images copyright © Shutterstock

Author's Note: This novel was originally published as "The Ghost of Hollow's Cove" under the name Kyle Butler in 2012.

Want to be the first to know about a new release? Subscribe to Jeff DeGordick's newsletter:
www.jeffdegordick.com/subscribe

Or say hello on my Facebook and Twitter page:
www.facebook.com/jeffdegordickauthor
www.twitter.com/jeffdegordick

I'm always happy to hear from my readers! Send me an email at:
jeff@jeffdegordick.com

Other books by Jeff DeGordick:
The Haunting of Bloodmoon House
The Witch of Halloween House
The Winterlake Haunting
The Ghosts of Jasper Bayou

— CHAPTER ONE —

THE CRIMSON SUNSET

He overlooked the bloody handprint stamped on the inside of the living room window as he headed up the driveway.

The setting sun cast its last rays against his back, warmly reminding him of the beautiful day he'd missed being cooped up in an office. He had a computer engineering job at a software company in Knoxville, Tennessee. It paid well, especially for someone still in his mid-thirties, though it had its compromises as well. But he had a lot to look forward to; because at the end of the day, he always remembered who he was: Mark Winters, family man. It was a humbling and joyful fact that kept his chin up day in and day out. But that was all about to change.

Mark fumbled around on his keychain for the house key. Sweat dripped from his short, light-brown hair. He wiped his face with the back of his hand, feeling two days worth of stubble scratch it. He remembered that he and his wife would have some free time on the weekend to do something fun with the kids. Maybe go rollerblading.

He unlocked the door and stepped into his cool house. He dropped his keys on the table in the hallway and kicked off his shoes. His feet relaxed.

Mark threw a glance at the brochure sitting on the table. *Hollow's Cove Lodge. Fishing, camping, swimming.* Maybe he should take the kids there on the weekend. His wife Theresa was never much for camping, but they could always stay in one of the clean-looking rooms advertised in the pictures.

What did that thing say, again? he asked himself, remembering picking it up in the morning on his way to work. He was running a little late and he tripped over the Incredible Hulk on his way out. It was one of Jamie's action figures, sitting on the front porch. When he bent down to pick it up, he saw the brochure lying beside it. He'd unfolded it and noted an odd message scrawled across the inside: "*The Black Warden returns*". It didn't look like part of the lodge's sales pitch. He didn't think anything of it at the time and tossed the brochure on the table then returned Jamie's action figure with his other toys in the rec room before heading off to work.

Standing in the hallway now, Mark shook his head at the brochure and unbuttoned his shirt. He went up the stairs to his bedroom at the end of the hall on the second floor. He plunked down on the bed and tossed his shirt aside, then began to remove his belt. He lay on the mattress in his undershirt, his arms stretched out to his sides.

It was this moment that he realized how quiet the house was. He listened for anything at all.

A HAUNTING AT HOLLOW'S COVE

The TV. The TV was on in the living room. What else?

Mark felt a chill roll down his spine. There were no other sounds at all. He sat up on the bed. He'd seen his wife's car in the driveway, and he knew his kids were home from school. The backyard crossed his mind, but the muffled screams and cackles of laughter were absent.

He ruminated on this then realized he was overthinking things. He leaned forward.

"Theresa?"

No answer.

Mark stood up, feeling his body stiffen. He walked down the hall to the stairs. A weakness invaded his legs, causing them to wobble and almost buckle with each step down. When he reached the bottom and stood once again at the front door, he had to take a moment to compose himself. The chattering sounds of the TV floated around the corner from the living room. He looked at the rec room at the end of the hallway. The only thing in view was part of a small canvas tent that the kids liked to use as their secret base of operations.

After steadying himself, he took a timid step forward and peeked into the living room.

The glowing images of a random cooking show danced across the TV screen. But the room was empty. Just the droning TV, an empty couch, and the splotch of red stained into the carpet.

Mark's heart sank. He staggered over to it to get a better look.

The next moments of his life took on a surreal quality that he would not entirely be able to recall afterward. He was helpless to do anything but look at the scene in horror as he saw drops of blood sprinkled over the carpet, leading from the large splotch toward the window looking out on the driveway.

He saw the handprint smeared on the glass. The words "Oh my God" tried to come out of his mouth, but a strained croak took its place. He didn't want to go on. He didn't want to see what was next. At that moment, he had the very simple wish that he didn't exist. He stood rooted in place for what seemed like an eternity. And then he was struck with a very betraying thought: *They could still be alive.*

Mark traced the trail of blood with his eyes as it wound across the carpet like a snake. It disappeared into the kitchen. He broke into a sprint, a sudden hope in him that not only was his family still alive, but that they could be saved if he acted quickly enough.

In the kitchen he saw the crimson trail lead around the oven and down a couple steps to the rec room. What his mind refused to acknowledge was that none of the blood looked fresh; it appeared as if it had been drying for hours.

But none of that mattered anymore when he rounded the corner into the rec room. As soon as he saw what was waiting for him, all his strength left him.

Theresa was lying facedown. In her arms she held their three-year-old daughter, Katelyn. Jamie, their five-year-old son, was halfway in the canvas tent, like he had tried to flee from their assailant. All of them were dead.

Mark frantically checked their bodies, trying to shake each of them back to life. When he accepted the fact that they were gone, he screamed. He only stopped screaming when he felt the urge to throw up. He sobbed uncontrollably in between howls of pain.

He gazed at the scene with watery eyes. Theresa's back was torn apart like she had been savaged by a wild animal. The cream carpet around her was stained a deep red. None of it made any sense. He couldn't understand a bit of it. He just knelt on the floor next to them, feeling his heart implode into itself.

And then he heard soft breathing behind him.

Mark froze. The hairs on the back of his neck stood up. His sobbing slowed into uneven sputters until eventually he was silent. He turned around.

The doorway to the kitchen stood before him. But there was no one there. Then soft footsteps played along the carpet runner in the hall.

Mark got to his feet and struggled to the doorway, his thoughts a tangled mess. The basement door in the middle of the hallway opened with a whine of the old hinges and footsteps clapped down the stairs. He didn't see who it was.

When he got to the open door, he stared down into the cold darkness. His bones rattled in fear and his teeth were set on edge as he wondered if he should go down. He flicked the light switch and a single dusty bulb hanging from a long black cord lit up the bottom of the stairs. Shadows stretched and writhed around the edges of its glow, concealing the unfinished basement and whoever lurked within it.

A cold sweat had broken out over Mark's skin. His fingers trembled and his throat was dry. The front door of his house—an escape—was in his mind. So was the phone to call the police. But the first thing he did was grab the chef's knife out of the block on the kitchen counter.

A quiet noise came from the basement.

Mark's numb hand lingered on the phone, but he removed it and walked to the edge of the stairs.

He strained his ears against the silence. He heard it again, and it sounded like the laughter of a child. But more than that, it sounded familiar.

Confusion mixed with the pain as he stared into the dark. He lingered another moment, then he descended the stairs. The cold air intensified, more than usual, it seemed. The knife shook in his grip.

When he reached the bottom of the stairs, Mark looked around. The dim light bulb highlighted a doorway to his left and only hinted at the shadows beyond it. The laughter had quieted, but he could hear the same soft breathing as he had upstairs coming from the room ahead.

Short, stilted breaths dragged in and out of Mark's lungs. He entered the darkness, pointing the knife in front of him. The basement was so cold. His hand patted the wall for the light switch, but before he found it he saw the killer in the darkness and the knife fell from his hand and clattered on the cement floor.

"*Oh Jesus*," he said.

The killer was standing at the other side of the room, and somehow Mark could see him through the darkness, like a glow was emanating from his body. But the thing that scared Mark the most was how small the murderer was, no bigger than a little boy. And when the boy turned around, Mark nearly fainted.

It was his son, Jamie. Aside from his ghostly glow, there was something off about his appearance that Mark couldn't place. But there was no mistaking him.

He tried to reconcile what he saw upstairs to what he was seeing now, but he couldn't. He opened his mouth to say something, but the words didn't come out. He could only watch his son in awe.

And just as suddenly as Jamie had come into view, he faded into the ether and left Mark alone in the dark.

— CHAPTER TWO —

NIGHT TERRORS

The detective's office in the police department's homicide division was very cold. Mark tried to reason that this was why he was shivering, but the truth was that he hadn't been able to stop since the police took him from the crime scene.

His home, a crime scene. It was every father's worst nightmare, and he couldn't begin to understand why it happened to him. He couldn't understand a lot of things about what happened today. The police had been quick to call his office and run his alibi to rule him out as the murderer, but he could feel the suspicion in the air.

"Mr. Winters?"

Mark looked up and fidgeted in his seat. The steely gaze of Detective Drucker fixed on him.

"Um, yes, I went downstairs after that," Mark said.

"Because you heard a noise?"

"No..." Mark glanced at his feet then scanned his eyes blankly across the room. Ever since finding his family when he came home, he couldn't concentrate on anything. "...I went downstairs because I *didn't* hear anything. My wife and kids should have been home, so that's why I..." His attention got lost in a fire safety poster on the wall.

"I see," Drucker said. "And you mentioned earlier that the front door was locked when you came home?"

"Yes."

"Do you know if any keys to your home were missing? We found one in your wife's pocket. How many others did you have?"

"None. She had the only other one."

"Did you lock any doors or windows after you came home?" Uncertainty rose in the detective's voice. His mind was racing, trying to solve a puzzle that had the wrong pieces.

Mark met his gaze again. "No. I just unlocked the front door when I came in. That was it."

"And no one else had a key? A friend or something?"

"No."

Drucker leaned forward and offered a weak smile. "There's just something I'm not quite getting." A cold look spread across his face. "The murders took place sometime in the middle of the day while you were at work. And when you got home, all the doors to the house were locked, all the windows were locked, no keys were missing. No sign of forced entry. After my men did a search, no one else was found in or around your home."

The sight of his ghostly son flashed in his mind. Mark had lied and said he didn't see anyone. Who would believe him? He didn't believe in ghosts either, but he knew what he saw.

"Yet somehow the killer was able to exit the house with no key and leave everything locked," Drucker continued. He looked at Mark with arising suspicion. Mark looked at him with blank eyes; the eyes of a man who wasn't there anymore.

The detective eased his gaze. "Listen, Mr. Winters... I know you want answers as much as we do, but we can't give you those answers if you're being evasive about this."

"I don't know what to tell you," Mark said. For the first time in his life, he felt utterly hopeless.

Drucker looked at him with pity. He knew Mark was hiding something, but at the same time, Mark didn't strike him as the kind of person who would have anything to do with this kind of tragedy.

The detective sighed. "Do you or your family have any enemies?" he asked. "Any bad debts?"

Mark shook his head. "None." He thought of the cryptic message written on the brochure he found that morning: "*The Black Warden returns*". It looked like a deliberate message sent to him, but he was completely in the dark about its meaning. And of what significance was Hollow's Cove, the fishing lodge the brochure was advertising? He didn't know, but the name had a ring to it, like it was somehow familiar to him.

A clerk came into the office and handed Drucker a file, saying a few words that Mark was too distracted to hear. The detective nodded and leafed through it. A uniformed officer stood in the doorway.

"It looks like this is all we need, Mr. Winters," Drucker said. "Officer Caldwell over here will work with you on where to go from here." He motioned to the door. "In the meantime, we'll do everything we can to figure this one out. I'm truly sorry about what happened to your family." He stood and shook Mark's hand. Just as Mark turned to leave, he spoke up: "Oh, Mr. Winters?"

Mark turned.

"We may have some more questions over the coming days, so don't leave town, okay?"

"Nowhere to go," Mark said absently. But his mind was already there: Hollow's Cove.

— — —

Mark found a serviceable motel on the edge of Knoxville to stay in for the night. Returning home certainly wasn't an option; even if the police weren't still picking over the house for clues, it would be the last place on Earth he would want to stay right now.

The Rest Easy's rooms were reasonably clean, its beds soft and its surrounding areas quiet. As Mark sat on the edge of his queen-sized bed, he almost wished his neighbors would make some noise; ever since the murders, his brain rattled around his head restlessly, creating an unbearable noise.

He kept himself busy by obsessively thinking about that lodge out in the woods of Clemington, South Carolina. The brochure painted Clemington as a small town without much of anything other than beautiful scenery and quiet vacationing spots. He didn't know anything about it himself as he'd never been there before. As far as he could remember, he'd never even crossed the border into South Carolina in his life.

Then why was that damn lodge so familiar? He thought back to when he picked up the brochure off his porch that morning and looked through it. The big images laid out over the pages came back to him, as vivid as when he first saw them. The main picture on the front showed a nice-looking two-story lodge sitting in the middle of otherwise undeveloped forest. A small parking lot sat in front, filled with cars. Business must usually be booming there, he figured.

He recalled that cryptic message written inside again. Who was the Black Warden? What kind of a name was that anyway? He considered that the brochure had been sent to the wrong address, but the sight of it sitting on his doorstep seemed a little too deliberate to be an accident.

He thought of the other pictures. There had been one in particular he couldn't get off his mind: it showed a lake extending out from the back of the lodge, its shore forming it into a rounded cove before connecting to the rest of the body of water in the distance. And at the back of the cove was a small island floating in the water that looked entirely undeveloped. Its simple appearance haunted him. He didn't know why.

Mark shook his head violently as if to loosen the images from his brain. He stood up and walked around the room, restless. He stopped at the window, peeked through the curtains at the completely uninteresting view, then continued pacing.

The silence in the room was unnerving. He turned on the TV and forced himself to watch it. As he did, the droning sounds of that cooking show playing on his TV at home crept into his head. He turned the TV off and sat on the edge of the bed, resting his face in his hands. He sobbed and let the tears run through his fingers. He continued this for several minutes until finally spinning around and collapsing on the bed. He fell asleep almost immediately.

— — —

Mark passed into a hazy dream. He was standing in front of the lodge at Hollow's Cove. The summer air was sticky. There was almost a smokiness to it. The parking lot in front of him was peppered with cars and trucks. Unspoiled woodland stretched out on either side of it. There was a path leading around the left side of the lodge down a hill, wrapping around to the grounds at the back. He couldn't see it from where he was standing, but the lake was down there. Lake Keowee. The name popped into his head as if he'd known it all his life.

A small boy ran past him toward the lodge. To his surprise, it was Jamie. But it wasn't the glowing, pale-skinned boy from the basement; it was his flesh and blood son that he'd known for the last five years. Looking at him now, he looked slightly different. Mark couldn't place what it was, but there was something off about his appearance. Maybe his hair was a bit longer, or maybe it was the angle Mark was standing at.

Jamie headed for the path leading around the lodge. Mark tried to say something but discovered he was paralyzed with the inability to speak. In fact, he couldn't even go after Jamie; it was as if he were rooted to the spot. Suddenly, Jamie was out of sight.

Now Mark was standing on a barren trail in the midst of very unnatural woods. The dense trees were blackened, twisting and spreading in ways they shouldn't. The soil under him was ashy and unsuitable for cultivating life. The air was still and very cold. He felt himself shiver. There were no noises either. No animals or insects in sight. By all appearances, the entire forest around him was dead.

A windowless cabin stood at the end of the trail in front of him. It looked as though it didn't belong where it was. The trail just seemed to end there, with wooded hills all around it. A cabin with no view, no purpose, no reason to be there. But there it stood, a shabby structure built of darkened, splintering wood. A set of steps rose up to a porch that stretched across the front of the small building. At the top of the steps was a closed door.

A HAUNTING AT HOLLOW'S COVE

A terrifying scream came from inside the cabin. It sounded like Jamie. He screamed over and over again, each one more violent. The terror and agony in his voice was incredible. After a few moments, the screaming stopped, replaced by a deafening silence. Mark could feel something change inside the cabin; something dreadful was born there. And it wanted to get out.

A chill ran up his spine as he stood rooted to the spot, unable to do anything but look. Panic swelled inside him. His eyes widened and his body trembled. The cabin seemed to leer at him. He didn't know what was in there; he only knew that something incredibly *bad* was inside that cabin's walls. Something that could never be let out.

Then Mark felt himself moving closer to it. He was powerless to stop the motion as his feet slid across the ground. He could feel the presence in the cabin grow in strength the closer he got. He tried to look away but his head was stuck. He wanted to close his eyes, but the sheer terror he felt kept them wide open.

The cabin was only a few feet away now. He tried to lean back and dig his heels into the dirt, but still he slid toward it. The door of the nightmarish structure became bigger and bigger. It was the only thing keeping the horrible thing inside away from him.

Mark's body was dragged up the steps, one by one. His mind teetered on the brink of insanity. His hands gripped the railing on either side of the steps with incredible strength, but still he was slipping. His fingernails dug into the wood, peeling thin strips from the boards.

He could hear the thing inside the cabin scratching the other side of the door, trying to get out. Mark's body was pulled up the last step and onto the porch. *No! NOOO!* his mind cried. His body finally came to rest before the door. The scratching stopped. Mark whimpered helplessly.

Then the doorknob slowly turned and the door opened, revealing blackness behind it. Mark stood, staring into the dark, tears streaming down his face. He felt like a little child about to be devoured.

The image burned into his memory, never to be forgotten: an infinite blackness; the most terrible thing standing in it, staring back.

— CHAPTER THREE —

HOLLOW'S COVE

Mark stood in his driveway. The afternoon sun blistered overhead. He was home, where this nightmare started. He so badly wanted to just walk inside and see his family. His mind was still reeling trying to comprehend why he couldn't do that.

He took a couple slow steps up the driveway. All of his senses seemed to be heightened, and he paid careful attention to the feel of the hot sun, the soft breeze on his skin, the quiet sounds of the suburban neighborhood. He tried to remember the exact sensations he felt the day before when he came home from work. He thought that if he could feel that, it would be like going back to a time before this terrible tragedy happened.

He walked past the living room window with the bloody handprint still smeared on it. His face screwed up and he tried not to burst into tears.

He stopped at the door and ran his fingers along the yellow police sticker taped to the jamb. He knew he'd be in big trouble if he was caught going inside, but he needed to get a couple things, and he wouldn't be long. He pulled his keys out of his pocket and unlocked the door. Mark gripped the doorknob and paused. His emotions needed to be in check before he attempted to walk inside. He knew that if he wasn't careful, he might have a nervous breakdown right in the front hallway.

With a deep breath, he turned the handle and pushed the door open, breaking the police sticker's seal. As he stepped inside, the rec room at the end of the hall tried to get his attention. He looked down at his feet and tried focusing on his shoelaces as he quickly shut the door behind him. The house stunk of chemicals and strange fluorescent sprays covered parts of the carpets and walls. He didn't look at any of it. Before he had any time to think, he went upstairs, taking the steps two at a time. When he was in his bedroom, he grabbed a small piece of luggage out of the closet and tossed it on the bed. He pulled out shirts, pants, socks and underwear and packed it into the luggage. When he finished, there was complete silence in the house. It was like an oppressive force, trying to invade his ears. He shook the feeling off and moved to the bathroom.

Packing all his toiletries, Mark zipped up the luggage and began to leave his bedroom. He paused at the doorway and looked over his shoulder. A framed picture of him and his family sat on the nightstand next to the bed. All four of them were smiling at the camera with a lopsided sand castle in front of them and rolling waves behind. He turned back and grabbed it.

A HAUNTING AT HOLLOW'S COVE

A wave of sadness suddenly overtook him. He faltered and sat down on the bed. Tears worked their way out of his eyes, but he fought with every ounce of his strength not to let this happen to him now; he knew if he stayed in this house any longer, much worse things would happen.

He pushed himself off the bed with his luggage in tow and took long strides for the stairs. Now all he needed was the most important thing he came for, then he would be on his way. When he was back in the front hall downstairs, he swiped the Hollow's Cove brochure off the table and walked out the front door, slamming it behind him.

A stilted breath shot out of his lungs. He took a few moments to try and work out all of the stifling feelings that he felt inside the house.

He locked the door then looked mournfully at the broken police sticker. They would know he was here. He glanced over at the garden in front of the house and saw a small decorative rock that his wife had placed there. The neighborhood was quiet and there was no one else on the street or in front of their homes. Mark's eyes scanned over the windows of each house, looking for bodies watching him. But he found no one.

He picked up the rock and turned to the window with the dried handprint. His lips peeling back into a snarl, he pivoted and hurled it through the glass. It shattered, and then that horrible sight was gone.

Before anyone could investigate the sudden noise, he disappeared.

— — —

The cab ride only took a few hours before he reached Clemington. So far, the South Carolinian weather didn't seem much different from the weather back in Knoxville, besides the fact that a stiff breeze raked through the air.

Mark paid the cab driver and took his piece of luggage. He watched as the cab sped off down the dirt road, winding around the corner and disappearing from sight. He turned and beheld the same image from the front of the brochure. Well, almost. The two-story lodge stood before him, but it didn't quite look as beautiful as it did in the picture. It was significantly more aged up-close, like the weather had done a number on it. The wood was moldy and cracked in places and the shingles on the roof were worn. The parking lot in front of the lodge was entirely empty except for two pickup trucks and a car. Maybe business wasn't quite booming after all. There was a path to the left of the lodge that wrapped around and out of sight, supposedly down to the main grounds in the back. It was just like it had been in his dream the night before.

He suddenly looked around, expecting to see his son running around somewhere. When it didn't happen, he felt a pang of sadness.

He headed for the front doors. A bell above them jangled as he walked inside. The small room before him looked just like he thought a fishing lodge might. All the walls, ceilings and floors were made from finished wood, with sprawling rugs and fishing adornments on the walls. The wall to his left was filled with mounted picture frames, most of them depicting people holding fish, some of people in boats or simply hanging around the lodge. Some were just pictures of what looked like the surrounding scenery.

A large oak reception desk sat in front of him. In the corner behind it, the wall opened up into a hallway. Mark heard faint voices coming from it.

He approached the desk and tapped the service bell. The bell dinged and he waited for someone to come. While he waited, his eyes scanned the desk. A messy pile of papers and forms littered the top. There was a little stand that held a few Hollow's Cove-branded matchbooks. He picked one up, turning it over in his fingers, then he stuffed it in his wallet.

Still no one came to greet him and still he could hear the faint voices of people talking and laughing. He walked over to the other side of the room where a trophy case was mounted to the wall. A wide range of trophies sat inside from small ones to large, multi-tiered ones. Most appeared to be for fishing, but there were a few odd ones out: a couple for baseball; a couple for different football tournaments; one for something about camping.

He felt the weight of his luggage tugging down on his increasingly strained arm. He shifted his weight then let out an impatient sigh. He turned and walked past the reception desk and entered the hallway. Just then, a slim black man with salt and pepper hair walked toward him with a slight limp. He wore an unbuttoned shirt with a thin white undershirt beneath. As the man reached him, he put the toothpick he was holding between his teeth and outstretched his arm.

"The name's Felix," he said with a grin.

Mark shifted his luggage and shook Felix's hand. "I'm Mark."

"What can I do for you today, Mark?"

Just as he was about to answer, Felix motioned for him to come back into the reception area. He took his spot behind the desk and stretched his hands out on it.

Mark put down his luggage and reached for his back pocket. He pulled out the brochure and placed it on the desk. Felix looked down at it in confusion and picked it up.

"This brochure was sent to me yesterday morning," Mark said. "I was hoping you could tell me a little bit about it."

Felix eyed the front of it and adjusted the toothpick in his teeth. "Well, Mark, I can tell you that this particular brochure hasn't been distributed in a number of years."

Mark drew closer to the desk. "How many years?"

Felix looked up, searching the corners of his memory. "I'd say somewhere between two to three decades ago."

"*Decades?*" Mark repeated in disbelief.

"That's right. Tell me... where on Earth did you get this old thing?"

"That's what I'm trying to figure out," Mark replied. "Like I said, it was sent to me yesterday. I found it on my doorstep. Being that it's a brochure for this place, I figured that it was sent from here."

Felix simply shook his head, flipping the brochure over and looking at the back.

"Are you the owner of this place?" Mark asked.

"Thirty years this summer."

Mark leaned on the desk, thinking very hard about who would have sent a brochure that old to him. There must have been a reason why it was that one and not a more recent one.

"What's this?" Felix asked. He had the brochure spread open, looking at something in the middle.

"The Black Warden returns?" Mark asked.

Felix looked up at him. His eyes had a very hard edge to them. "What the hell is this about, mister?"

"Not a clue. I was kind of hoping you would know."

"You seem to be hoping for a lot of strange things."

Mark let out a deep breath and straightened up. He reached for the brochure and Felix handed it to him.

"Well, I guess I'll take a room, then," he said.

Felix's brow furrowed. "Listen, what's this all about? I don't need any strangers poking around and causing trouble."

"No trouble," Mark promised. "You won't even know I'm here. I'm just trying to figure out what's going on."

"Over a brochure?" Felix asked. "What difference does it make?"

"It's personal."

Felix looked at him for a long moment, then he relented. "You know, Mark, this is our rainy season. We don't get a lot of people staying here around this time."

"I don't mind a little rain," Mark said.

Felix spoke slowly as if Mark didn't quite understand: "It's not just going to be a little rain. There's supposed to be a bad storm coming. Worse than this side of the woods has seen in years. Are you sure you want to stay?"

Mark didn't even process Felix's warning. "Yes. I do."

Felix shrugged. "All right, one room coming right up." He reached into a drawer and pulled out a hardback ledger. He flipped through most of it and stopped on a page, placing his pen to the surface. He looked up at Mark. "Last name?"

"Winters."

"Winters," Felix repeated as he scribbled it down. "And how long will you be staying, Mr. Winters?"

"As long as I need."

A curious look spread over Felix's face. "Okay..." He jotted something down beside Mark's name and closed the book. "I'm going to need your credit card number ahead of time, then."

Mark pulled out his wallet and slid his credit card to him. Felix wrote down the number on a separate piece of paper, tucked it away in a file, then gave Mark the card back.

"All right then, Mark, let me show you to your room." He stepped out from behind the desk and gestured for Mark to follow him. They went down the hallway, which opened up into a large lounge area. To their left they passed two men sitting at a bar, talking. An old-fashioned jukebox, a pool table, a couch and some chairs also furnished the room. On their right, the lounge connected to a small library filled with hundreds of books. They continued on past a staircase that led to the second floor, and went into another hallway.

Felix poked his toothpick around in his mouth as he twisted his body to talk to Mark. "I cook breakfast every morning, lunch in the afternoons, and supper every day. It's all complimentary, but drinks at the bar will cost you extra."

They entered the first door on their left.

"I don't drink," Mark said.

"Fishing boats are also complimentary, but I don't get the feeling you're here for the fishing."

Mark offered a weak smile.

"Well, this is your room," Felix said.

Mark looked around. It was a small room with a single bed, a writing desk, a small freezer and an attached bathroom. There didn't appear to be any frills, but he didn't need them. "Thanks," he said.

"Don't mention it. There are a couple guys out in the lounge I'll introduce you to once you get settled."

"Looking forward to it," Mark said.

Felix limped out of the room, closing the door behind him.

Mark set his luggage down on the bed and sat next to it. He fished through it and pulled out the framed picture of his family and set it on the writing table. He stared at it and held back a sob. He stood up and walked around his bed to the large window over it. The cove stood right in front of him, with wooded hills stretching around either side of it. Up the hill on the left, he spotted a two-story house deep in the woods. The gravel trail that wrapped around the side of the lodge extended across his window, leading to the docks on the edge of the water. To the right of them was a shabby old boathouse. And beyond that the terrain crept up a hill on the right, leading to a small cottage overlooking the lake.

The island sat at the back of the cove. All Mark could make out from this distance was a bit of shore. It extended up a shallow hill, concealing the trail beyond. The rest of the island was hard to see; even in the daytime a blanket of shadows shrouded it.

He felt a deep chill enter the room. He stared at the island. The island stared back.

— CHAPTER FOUR —

Meeting the Locals

Mark left his room about two hours later. As he walked into the lounge, he saw that everyone was gone. To the right of the bar, the wall cut away and led into another room. The faint sounds of talking floated out from it.

Dark clouds had formed since he first checked in at three in the afternoon. The grounds outside the lounge's windows were slick with fresh rain. The lake seemed to take on an ominous appearance, with the island in the background looking almost sinister. Fortunately, the rain was light and it looked like the storm Felix promised hadn't hit yet.

Mark walked around the bar and into what was quite obviously the lodge's dining room. Felix was sitting down at a big table with the same two men who were sitting at the bar earlier. Plates of food and bottles of beer sat in front of them. They all paused their conversation and looked up at Mark in unison, making him feel a little awkward. Felix sat up, quick to break the tension.

"Have a seat, Mark, have a seat."

Mark nodded and sat beside a tall, white-haired man.

Before he'd left his room, he made sure he thoroughly wiped his eyes, but there was still a tinge of red to them. Embarrassed, Felix looked down at his beer. He tried to pretend that he hadn't heard Mark crying in his room, but Mark noticed his sheepish look.

"You weren't choppin' onions, were ya?" the man sitting across from Mark asked him. He was bulky, dressed in a collared shirt with the sleeves rolled up and a dirty pair of jeans. A purple trucker's hat capped his head with a logo that read "Southern Anglers Challenge".

Mark suddenly felt very self-conscious. It took him two hours to finally drag himself out of his room and join the rest of society, and now he just wished he stayed there forever.

He rubbed his eyes. "Allergies. Not quite used to this neck of the woods."

The man across from him nodded slowly with a smirk.

Felix cleared his throat. "Mark, let me introduce you to these guys. They're a couple of regulars." He leaned forward in his chair and nodded toward the tall man beside Mark. "This is Jerry."

Jerry turned in his seat and shook Mark's hand. "Good to meet you!" he said. He looked to be in his late sixties with his thick, white hair combed to the side. He wore very large, square glasses and a nearly orange tan radiated from his skin. He was quite thin for his height, but the jowls on his face hung down quite a bit, and coupled with his mouth that always hung open a little, it gave him a bewildered look. Mark noticed Jerry's gold watch and figured if that wasn't a dead giveaway that the man was retired, his slacks and polo top were.

"Good to meet you, too," Mark said.

Felix swiveled in his seat and motioned toward the bulky man beside him. "Mark, this is Pete."

Pete gave Mark a dry nod. Mark returned the courtesy.

"Let me grab you some supper," Felix said to Mark, standing suddenly. He turned and disappeared through a pair of batwing doors behind him.

An uncomfortable silence held in the air. Mark and Pete were aware of it, but Jerry seemed to be completely oblivious, happily eating his supper.

"So Mark, what brings you here this time of year?" Jerry asked.

Mark tried to think of what to say. He came to this lodge to find his family's killer. And who the Black Warden was. And why he started seeing his dead son.

"I, uh..." he started, then leaned his face on his hand, stumped. He was in such a rush to get here that he didn't think he would have to use simple people skills.

Pete gave a smug laugh. "We don't get too many people of your type around here in this season."

"What type is that?" Mark asked indignantly.

"Oh, how do I put this? You know... well, the *sensitive* type. Judging by the ring on your finger, I'd normally say you were married, but married men don't book themselves a room in some lodge to cry. So I guess that puts you at recently separated." The smirk on Pete's face spread a little wider. "How am I doin' so far?"

Anger began to swell in Mark. He so badly wanted to slug Pete right in the face, but he restrained himself.

"Let me put it plainly for you, Mark. We regulars like the down time around here when we can get it. You're not gonna find much hospitality around here."

"Pete! What do you think you're doing, for cryin' out loud?" Jerry said, finally seeming to catch on to the rising tension in the room.

As if in answer to the escalating situation, the bat-wing doors flew open and Felix pressed through, holding a plate of food in one hand and a beer in the other. He set each one down in front of Mark and sat down again. Mark looked at the beer and was about to remind Felix that he didn't drink, but he looked at Pete's coy smile and thought better of it.

"So Mark, remind me... What brings you around here?" Felix asked. His brain had been on autopilot and his first encounter with Mark slipped his mind for a se-cond. Before he could ask a different question, Pete looked from Felix to Mark, beaming.

"Our good friend Mark was just about to answer that, as a matter of fact," Pete said.

"I think our good friend Peter has had a little too much to drink already," Mark said.

Felix shot Pete a look, and Mark got the feeling that Pete's behavior was pretty common. Everyone dropped the issue after that and moved down to an only slightly awkward tension as they ate.

Mark dug into his grilled chicken and baked potato. As he ate, he left his warming beer untouched, hoping no one would notice.

"I spotted your shiny gold watch, Jerry," Mark said. "Where'd you used to work?" He thought that if he started asking the questions, it wouldn't leave room for anyone to ask him any.

Jerry's ears perked up. "Oh! I used to work at Milliken over in Spartanburg. I worked there for forty-five years until I retired back in '14."

"Milliken... I've heard of that," Mark said. "What was it like working there?"

Felix seemed to tense up as he asked the question. Even Pete was shaking his head at him, his eyes wide.

"Oh, I tell you! It was a great place!" Jerry chimed.

Mark didn't realize his mistake until it was too late. The three of them spent the next half hour listening to Jerry explicitly go over all the details of life at Milliken & Company. He spared no detail in his account, even talking about the color of their punch cards and how expertly-measured the parking spaces were. By the time he was finished talking, Mark's plate was clean and Pete's head was facedown on the table.

Noticing the new silence, Pete poked his head up. He looked around in a daze and spotted Mark's unopened beer.

"Mark, if you're not gonna drink that, you're gonna have to be a gentleman and pass it to me. I really need it about now."

Mark slid the beer over to Pete who cracked it open and guzzled it. Felix rubbed his eyes and began shifting in his seat. Jerry was still smiling away, happy that Mark was interested in his work.

Just then, a set of doors in the lounge opened and a tall, somewhat portly man walked in. He glanced around the lounge, let his face dissolve into a frown, then looked at his watch. He turned his head to the right and saw everyone sitting in the dining room. He raised his head in recognition, making a small triumphant sound. The man said a quick hello and strolled into the dining room, taking a seat on Mark's other side. He looked to be in his early seventies, with wild, white hair haphazardly tucked under a straw hat. The rest of his appearance didn't look much less disheveled, with stains covering his long-sleeved shirt and khaki pants in various places.

"Hector, nice of you to join us," Felix said.

"Just thought I'd stop in and say hello." Hector's voice was surprisingly squirrelly for a man of his size and he had a nervous demeanor to him, as if he thought someone might strike out at him. He turned his head and looked at Mark, then shot a confused look at Felix as if he couldn't comprehend an actual customer in the lodge.

"Hector, this is Mark. He's an out-of-towner staying here for a few days," Felix said. He nodded his head toward the right side of the lake. "Hector has a cottage overlooking the lake just up the hill over there."

"I don't see many people staying here during the rainy season," Hector said, sizing up Mark. "The thunderstorms usually scare away the tourists, you see."

"I'm not here for the fishing," Mark said. He regretted the words before they even finished coming out of his mouth.

Hector looked confused, and Felix gave him a sly shake of his head. Hector considered his expression for a moment, then shook his own head, as if to get the thought out.

"How long have you had the cottage?" Mark asked.

"Oh, I've lived there all my life, actually. My father built it back when I was a young boy. He passed when I was still a strapping lad and left it to me in his will. I decided to keep the place."

"Would you like any supper, Hector?" Felix asked. "I've got some chicken on tonight."

Hector considered this for a moment, then asked: "Do you have any potatoes?"

Felix nodded and disappeared through the batwing doors. A few moments later, he returned with a baked potato. Hector took some butter from the table and began slathering the inside of it.

"Hear anything good in town lately, Hector?" Jerry asked.

"Sorry to disappoint you, my boy. A broken sewer pipe under Don's Market is the best I've got right now."

Jerry looked down in disappointment.

"You'll find these two bickering like a couple of old ninnies anytime they get together," Pete said to Mark.

"Oh, come off it!" Jerry said, perturbed.

"So what about you, Pete?" Mark said. "Why do you hang around here all the time?"

"'Cause Felix hasn't made me pay up on my tab yet."

Felix shot Pete a sour look. Hector sat listening contently, still buttering his potato.

"I see I'm not the only one who can dodge a question," Mark said with a smile.

"I like the fishing."

"I thought people didn't fish in the rainy season."

"*Real* men fish anytime they choose. Out-of-towners—especially the delicate ones—get scared off by a little rain. Real fishermen know the bite's the best right before a storm."

Felix chimed in. "Old Pete here's got a farm just uptown a bit. He's got two strong, young boys to take on some of the workload, so he's got plenty of time to spare these days. Spends his free time fishing here as much as he can get."

Pete nodded in approval.

Hector finally started digging into his cooling potato. "Is this your first time in Clemington, Mark?"

"Yeah."

"Whereabouts are you from?"

"I'm from Knoxville over in Tennessee."

"Now why would a man from Tennessee come all the way to this quiet little fishing lodge in Clemington if not for the fishing?" Hector regarded Mark with genuine curiosity. "You are a very strange man, indeed."

"I don't mean to create any great mysteries," Mark said, "but by the same token, I hope you don't mind if I say it's personal."

"Oh! Not at all, my boy. Please forgive the intrusion." Hector looked slightly afraid for asking the question. He nervously folded his hands into each other then continued working on his potato. When he finally finished it, he excused himself from the table.

"Well, it was a pleasure to see you all this evening," he said. "You too, Mark." Hector nodded at him. "Thanks for the food, Felix."

"No problem," Felix replied.

Hector turned and left through the lounge doors, clamping a hand on top of his straw hat to make sure the wind didn't take it off.

So these are the locals, huh? Mark thought. They were an eclectic bunch, but nothing too out of the ordinary. He was still completely in the dark about what he was doing here and where to go next. But he wouldn't let himself come to a dead end with this. He promised Felix he wouldn't cause trouble, but that didn't mean he couldn't dig a little.

— CHAPTER FIVE —

Trading Stories

Mark, Jerry and Pete moved to the bar in the lounge while Felix cleaned up the dishes. When he was finished, he came out and joined them, acting as bartender. Pete and Jerry were simple guys, so he never had to do anything more complicated than pull a beer from the fridge.

Pete stood up and walked over to the jukebox sitting next to the lounge doors. He slapped a button and returned to his seat. The jukebox's lights came on and the lively sounds of "Up Around the Bend" by Creedence Clearwater Revival came on.

Felix slid two beers across the bar top to Jerry and Pete. He pulled one out for himself and was about to grab another one for Mark, but he stayed his hand. Instead he turned around and poured Mark a glass of water, furnishing a slice of lemon on the edge. Mark thanked Felix and gratefully drank from the tall glass.

As the drinks and music flowed, everyone eased into a more comfortable state. Pete downed beer after beer, slumping lower against the bar as the night went on. Jerry seemed to get even friendlier than he normally was. He leaned over and wrapped an arm around Mark's shoulders.

"Listen, Mark... don't take no offense to what Pete said earlier. He doesn't mean anything by it."

"That's just Pete's way of saying hello," Felix added as he reached in his breast pocket and pulled out a toothpick, sticking it between his teeth. "As long as Pete's got a beer in hand and the jukebox on, he's happier than a fly on dog shit!"

Everyone laughed except for Pete who drank deeply from his beer. He seemed to perk up again when "Radar Love" by Golden Earring drifted out of the jukebox.

As Mark sat there, he was suddenly overcome by a feeling he wasn't familiar with in the last two days: it was happiness. He realized that sitting in the company of near strangers in a foreign place was actually taking his mind off his family. He was grateful for that. As much of an asshole as Pete seemed to be some of the time, he was appreciative of his company.

The four of them hung out at the bar, drinking, listening to classic rock and trading stories. Jerry ended up twice telling the same story of the time he and his late wife lost their dog. The songs pouring out of the jukebox measured the time as the day faded into night.

The sky outside became darker and darker, the clouds growing very heavy. A thick downpour pelted the grounds out the window.

"Shouldn't you be fishing about now, Pete?" Mark joked.

"Not in this weather, you dumbass." Pete was now so low to the bar that he was almost sipping his beer sideways.

"I thought real fishermen weren't afraid of a little rain," Mark goaded, perhaps a little too much.

Pete immediately rose from his stool, beer bottle in hand. Mark was just trying to get a friendly jab in, hoping to loosen him up a bit, but it had the opposite effect. Pete had a deadly look in his eyes, his nostrils flaring.

"Ease up, Pete," Felix warned.

Pete ignored him and took a drunken step toward Mark. "Wha'd you say to me?"

"I didn't mean to get you all riled up, Pete," Mark said. "Sit down."

"Don't tell me to fuggin' si'down," Pete slurred as he took another step forward. He smashed his beer bottle on the edge of the bar. Beer and brown glass flew. He continued toward Mark, brandishing the broken end at him.

"Pete, I'm warning you," Felix said, bending to reach under the bar for something.

Mark stood up and faced Pete.

"For God's sake, Pete, relax!" Jerry said, putting a hand on his shoulder.

Pete grabbed Jerry's hand and threw it off.

Felix straightened up, holding a shotgun. But it wasn't enough warning for Pete as he took a swing at Mark.

"Damn it, Pete!" Felix yelled. Frustrated, he put the shotgun down and limped out from behind the bar.

A HAUNTING AT HOLLOW'S COVE

Mark ducked the broken bottle and shoved Pete backwards. Pete stumbled and fell onto a barstool. Jerry tried to grab hold of him, but he wrestled his way out. As he got up, he lunged at Mark. Mark sidestepped out of the way and he drunkenly collided into the pool table, letting out a loud grunt. Mark leaned his weight on Pete's back, pinning him, then he grabbed Pete's wrist and slammed his hand on the edge of the table. The remainder of the bottle shattered in Pete's hand.

Pete let out a deep groan as blood began to pump out of his lacerated palm. His body slid down the pool table and slumped to the ground. Mark stepped back, immediately regretting what he'd done.

"I'm sorry," Mark croaked. "I didn't mean to hurt him."

Felix ignored him as he bent over Pete with a first aid kit. He checked to make sure he didn't have any pieces of glass stuck in his hand, then he tended to the wound. "Jerry, call an ambulance," he said.

Jerry nodded, staring at Pete in disbelief. He got up and walked over to a phone mounted on the wall behind the bar.

Mark stood there, watching Pete's sad figure curled up on the ground. He awkwardly held his hands by his waist, ashamed. Did he really hurt Pete so badly that he needed an ambulance? He suddenly felt that his welcome was wearing out.

A few minutes later, an ambulance showed up and took Pete away to the hospital. Jerry said that he would follow and make sure he ended up okay. Felix didn't even look at Mark the entire time the paramedics were there, and when they had finally left and it was just the two of them alone in the lounge, Mark felt a very thick presence in the air.

"Look, I'm really sorry about what happened," he said, holding his hands up in defense.

Felix broke into a laugh. "Don't sweat it. I'm the one who should be apologizing to you. It's not a very good business practice to have my customers attacked by the local drunks."

"Why do you keep him around if he just picks fights?" Mark asked.

"He's mostly the reason why I have any income at all in the off season. Jerry started hanging around here regularly a few years ago, but before that it was just Pete. Plus Pete's really not so bad." Felix took note of Mark's suspicious look. "You just gotta get to know him, that's all."

Felix started picking up pieces of broken glass. Mark offered his help and the two of them worked their way around the room cleaning up the mess. After they finished, they sat at the bar for the rest of the night, listening to the rain pounding on the windows. It was pitch-black outside, the clouds choking whatever moonlight tried to filter through.

"So are you going to tell me the real reason you're here anytime during your indefinite stay?" Felix asked.

Mark let out a half-hearted laugh. "I suppose I should," he said.

Felix leaned in, preparing himself for a great revelation.

"Yesterday I came home from work and found my family murdered."

Felix's jaw sank. When he didn't say anything, Mark continued.

"I have no idea who killed them." He closed his eyes. Visions of bloodstains on the floors and walls entered his mind. He heard the sound of childish laughter coming from the basement again.

"Christ," Felix said, darting his eyes back and forth. "I can't even imagine."

"Neither can I," Mark said, staring off into space. He thought of Jamie standing in the basement again, but knew better than to mention it. "I went over the events a hundred times in my head and the only thing out of place that whole day was the brochure that was on my porch. It's like someone wanted me to come here."

"'The Black Warden returns'," Felix recalled.

Mark looked at him. "Yeah. But I don't know what the hell that means. Are you sure you've never heard that phrase before? Never heard of a 'Black Warden'?"

Felix shook his head. "I wish I could help you. I really do. No man should have to go through that." He suddenly looked down, thinking. "You know, you should stop by Hector's place tomorrow and pay him a visit. He's got an ear for gossip and he's lived near this lodge his whole life, like he said."

"Thanks. I'll do that." Mark was grateful that he had some kind of lead, even if it was a small one. But he wasn't satisfied with it. "You said you've been here for thirty years?"

"That's right."

"Has anything significant ever happened here? Anything serious?"

"Well, there've been a few things." Felix thought for a moment. He reached into his pocket and popped another toothpick into his mouth, chomping on it and rearranging it with his tongue. "Three little boys were staying here one summer with their parents. They were playing out in the woods one day and they went missing. No one ever found them. That one happened a long time before I bought the place.

"There was one year where a man killed his little boy," he continued. He paused in thought again.

"There was also another time when a teenage girl drowned in the lake." He looked at Mark, content that he'd remembered everything.

Mark carefully listened as Felix mentioned each incident, hoping that one of them would somehow be similar to what happened to his family. But when Felix was finished, he was visibly disappointed.

"I'm really sorry I can't help you," Felix said. "Like I said, go see Hector tomorrow. He might be of more use than you think."

Mark nodded in appreciation, not wanting Felix to think that he took his hospitality for granted.

Felix leaned back and let out a long sigh. "I don't know about you, but I could really use a drink." He stood up and walked around the bar, grabbing a tumbler and a bottle of scotch. He returned to his stool and began pouring. "Are you sure you don't want a drink?" he asked. "You really look like you could use it."

Mark waved him away. When he opened his mouth, Felix spoke for him.

"You don't drink," he said.

"That's right."

"Any particular reason, if you don't mind my asking?"

"No, that's all right." Mark shifted in his seat. "My dad was an alcoholic. He was very abusive to me."

"Abusive to your mom, too?"

"My mom died in a car accident when I was three. I was an only child too, so I didn't have anyone to help me. It was just me and my father for all those years. I lived in fear every day. The times when he got so drunk that he just passed out for the whole day were the best. It didn't take much to upset him, either. He would always get very violent, very fast." Mark rubbed his temples. His head was starting to throb just thinking about it.

"But at least my dad did one thing right: he made me into the man I am today. When I got older, I promised myself that I would never turn into him. So I've never touched a single drop of alcohol. I ran away from home when I was fourteen and made it on my own ever since then. When I was sixteen, an old friend of my dad's called me and told me that he hanged himself. Every time I got any kind of success in life, I would always look back on my dad and think of how much better of a man I turned out to be than he did. Like I'd succeeded where he never could."

Tears rolled down Mark's face. "But I failed my family," he said. "I wasn't there when they needed me the most."

"Where were you?" Felix asked sympathetically.

"I was at work."

Felix put a hand on his shoulder. "Well then there was nothing you could do," he reasoned. "It wasn't your fault."

But Mark didn't look convinced.

"I know what it's like to lose your family," Felix said, trying to console him.

"Your family was killed?"

"No..." Felix looked away, wishing he had chosen different words. "I used to have a wife and a daughter, but I haven't seen them in a long time. I used to be the sheriff of Clemington back in the day, believe it or not."

"How long ago?" Mark asked.

"1985 was the last time I held the badge, thirty-two years ago. I was young at the time, but I was a real up-and-comer. I had nine good years as a deputy in this town and I got overwhelming support from the folks here when the sheriff's position was up for election. I was happily married to my wife and we had our beautiful daughter, Stephanie. And back then, I can honestly say that my wife was happily married to me." Felix lamented for a moment then drank his entire tumbler of scotch. He poured himself another.

"But things took a turn for the worse when I became sheriff," he continued. "I got caught up in a case—obsessed. I wasn't thinking straight; I should've known when to cut loose. All I got for my troubles was this bum leg," he said, patting his right knee. "After that, I couldn't do the job no more... had to step down. I took an injury pension and bought this lodge a couple years later as something to do."

Felix took a swig of scotch and stared at the bottom of the glass.

"You would think being retired would stop me." He laughed. "It didn't. I just wouldn't let it go. My wife became so fed up that she left with our daughter. That was thirty years ago, and now I don't have anything left. I'm just a tired old man who threw his life away." He emptied his glass.

"You haven't seen your daughter in thirty years?" Mark asked, stunned.

"That's right."

"Have you ever tried to contact her?"

"As a matter of fact, I did. She's grown into a woman. She has a son... I'm a grandpa," he said with a smile. "I decided the world wasn't gonna set things right for me, so I'm gonna set them right myself. Stephanie and I have been sending each other letters for the past little while. She seems to want to get to know me again. She invited me to my grandson's birthday next weekend. Little Jacob is going to be six."

"You must be pretty excited," Mark said.

"I'm counting the days. I told Stephanie I wouldn't miss it for the world. I told her that even though I've let her down plenty in the past, I'm a changed man."

"I'll bet she's counting down the days, too," Mark said. "It's going to be nice to see your daughter again," he said, somewhat sadly.

Felix's smile faded as he realized that he originally told Mark about his daughter to connect with him, but the only thing he did was remind him that he'll never see his family again.

He grunted and stood up. "Well, I think it's time I hit the hay."

"Yeah, me too," Mark said, getting up.

Felix limped up the staircase, grabbing the railing for support. When he was halfway up, he stopped and looked down at Mark.

"Are you sure you want to stay here?" he asked. "There's a really bad storm coming in."

Mark just stared at him.

"I don't think you'll enjoy your stay."

— CHAPTER SIX —

Midnight Observations

Mark finished brushing his teeth and walked back into his room. He looked at the clock radio sitting on the writing desk.

12:00.

He picked up the picture of his family and stroked his fingers across it, then put it back down. The light from the ceiling fixture bounced off the coverless window, making it impossible to see outside into the darkness.

Ready to go to bed, he walked over to the door and flipped off the lights, then walked to the window and looked outside.

The landscape was more visible now; the rain had finally stopped and the clouds parted, letting the moon shine its light through. It twinkled on the surface of the lake as gentle ripples moved about. The island stood at the back of the cove as a silhouette; a dark fortress in the night. The way it seemed to let no light shine upon it was very peculiar. Only the front shore was visible.

And the person standing on it.

Mark pressed his nose to the glass, trying to get as close of a look as he could.

A small fishing boat was dragged up on shore. Standing in front of it was a person dressed in what appeared to be a black cloak. Mark couldn't tell if this was actually the case or if the person was simply too shrouded in the darkness. The person bent over the boat and reached for something inside. After a few moments, they straightened up and cradled their arms like they were holding something, then walked up the hill and disappeared into the darkness.

Mark watched and waited, expecting something terrifying to happen. Why someone would be going to a pitch-black island in the middle of the night was beyond him.

The water from the lake gently rose up on shore, splashing the boat. As he stared at the darkness resting on the island, he had the chilling feeling that he was being watched. The odd feeling gripped him for a moment, then passed. He continued to look at the darkness, breathless.

A stiff breeze picked up and blew across the grounds. The trees in the woods all around the lake began to sway. But the silhouetted trees on the island remained still.

The darkness seemed to swell, growing larger and more potent. The island appeared to be getting bigger; more powerful. And just a moment later, the feeling passed. The island looked the same as it had before.

Mark let out a labored breath. There was still no sign of the person who had disappeared over the hill and into the darkness. The breeze seemed to die down and the trees straightened up. The waters of the lake calmed.

He looked over to Hector's cottage up the hill to the right. He remembered Felix's advice about talking to him. He decided he would visit Hector the next day after breakfast. Hopefully he could provide some kind of lead. If he couldn't, Mark had no idea what he would do. The thought of leaving the lodge empty-handed was unbearable.

He scanned the woods on the left side of the cove, darting his eyes between darkened trees. The large house stood deep in the woods. No light emitted from any of the windows, and Mark wondered whether the occupants of the house were simply asleep, or if the house had been abandoned. It was hard to see from this distance, but the house looked like it had seen better days. It carried an odd shape to it, as if a portion of the roof had started to sag.

The trees seemed to be densest around the house, thinning out as they led down toward the lodge. He traced the line of trees as they dotted their way down the landscape. His gaze jumped from tree to tree to man to tree.

His eyes flicked back and he knew why he'd felt like he was being watched before: the black silhouette of a man was standing in the woods beside a tree. He was very tall, and even though he was completely enveloped in darkness, Mark knew that the man was staring at him. The hairs stood up on the back of his neck. Even though he was in a pitch-black room, the unusually tall man's head pointed directly at him.

Mark shot his eyes up at the house deep in the woods. Could he be someone living in that house? The man wasn't too far away from it. Mark looked back at him. But he was gone. He looked around the woods, searching for the tall silhouette. He couldn't find him. Just when he looked away for a brief moment, the man had disappeared, almost as if he could not only see him in his dark room, but he could see exactly where his eyes were looking.

After another few seconds of searching the woods, the house, and the surrounding area, he began to think that maybe he'd hallucinated the man. Maybe he was too tired. Maybe his mental state hadn't quite been right since coming home from work the day before. Hell, he knew it hadn't.

He looked at the island on the lake again, expecting to see nothing on its shore; just a mirage for a crazed man.

The boat was still there, but the darkness offered no sign of the person in the black cloak.

A faint creaking noise sounded from somewhere in the lodge. Mark froze. It sounded like a door opening. The creak whined again and was followed by the sound of a door being snuggly shut.

A HAUNTING AT HOLLOW'S COVE

Floorboards started to creak somewhere in the lounge. The noises slowly made their way closer. The boards in the guest-rooms hallway groaned. The creaks were deliberate, slowly getting closer and closer to his door. A final floorboard groaned right outside of it.

He stood in his pitch-black room, defenseless. The door loomed at him, the only thing standing between him and the man from the woods. His mind flashed to the dream of standing in front of the cabin door as the thing on the other side scratched and clawed to get out.

Just then, a scratching sound came from the other side of the door. It was slow and almost seductive, scraping into the wood. Finally it stopped and a permeable silence crawled through the air.

Mark silently watched the door, waiting for something to happen. After what seemed like an eternity, he decided he should open it. The room had been dead silent for so long, he was starting to believe he'd imagined the scratching sound.

He slowly moved toward the door, the old floorboards groaning under his weight. Whatever was waiting for him on the other side did so in silence. Mark bunched his hand into a fist. He slowly turned the doorknob then pulled it forcefully.

The door swung open, revealing an empty hallway behind it.

Mark stood in stunned immobility. He was *sure* he heard someone on the other side of the door; he couldn't have been this crazy. He poked his head out, glancing left and right. Still, he saw nothing. He moved to the lounge, feeling vulnerable in the open. Moonlight came through the windows, fashioning everything inside with a pale glow. The only sound in the lodge was the ticking of a clock somewhere and the heavy beating of his heart.

He looked up the staircase leading to the second floor. The door to Felix's room was closed. There didn't appear to be anything out of the ordinary. He paused and listened closely for anything audible. But there was nothing. He wandered over to one of the windows and glanced at the woods, but there was no sign of the tall man.

Maybe he really *was* losing it—hearing noises in the dark, seeing people that weren't there.

When he was convinced that there was no one in the lodge after all, he shrugged to himself and returned to his room.

Just before he entered, a noise came from inside. It happened so quickly that he wasn't able to comprehend what it was, but he was positive he heard it. A thick silence followed, as if trying to once again convince him that he was crazy. His heart pounding furiously, he crept around the doorway and flicked the light on.

Empty.

He shut the door behind him then moved to the bathroom. Empty. He checked under the bed. Empty. He sighed and rubbed his eyes. He *was* tired. That was it. He just needed to get some rest and he would be okay in the morning. He turned off the light again. Just before he lay down, he took one last look out his window. The ominous house stood in the woods as a tight fear seeped through his veins.

Mark was now standing behind the lodge, on the path leading down to the docks. The hot sunlight covered his face and he raised an arm to shield his eyes. The sounds of nature were buzzing in the sticky summer air as a cool breeze rolled across the land. The pristine lake water sparkled, giving the whole cove a very lush, calming feeling. Down at the docks, an old rowboat bobbed in the water, tied to one of the wooden posts.

Laughter drifted from behind him, and he tried to turn around to find the source of it, but he once again found that he was immobilized, only able to watch what was happening in front of him.

A young boy ran past him down the path. He stopped partway and turned. It was Jamie. And again, it was the flesh and blood Jamie from his dream the night before. But still there was something off about his appearance, something that Mark still couldn't place.

Jamie looked at him and giggled. He waved his hand, motioning Mark to follow him, then continued running down the path.

Mark ran after him until they got to the docks. Jamie stopped and looked out over the water. Mark screeched to a halt. He tried to keep running, but his legs wouldn't move. He opened his mouth to call Jamie's name, but nothing came out.

Jamie stared over the lake, his head scanning from side to side. Suddenly, his gaze stopped on something that captured his interest.

It was the island.

He turned around and looked at Mark, giggling again, then ran across the dock.

Jamie, wait! Mark tried to say, his mouth stupidly hanging open. His legs allowed him to follow this time.

The rowboat tied to the end gently bumped into the dock as the water shifted about beneath it. Jamie hopped into the boat and motioned for Mark to join him.

Mark looked from Jamie to the island and back again. Fear blanketed him at the thought of going there. This time he didn't want to walk, but his legs were moving automatically. He fought against it, but he was powerless to stop himself. He knew where this ended and he would give anything in the world to prevent it. That terrible cabin was on that island. He was sure of it.

His body moved into the shabby rowboat and sat across from Jamie. The island was perched just over Jamie's shoulder and Mark could see two very juxtaposing things: his sweet and innocent son smiling, not knowing what was about to happen to them; and the most terrible thing, sitting out on the water like a soulless monolith.

To his horror, his hands untied the rope and grabbed an oar, dipping it into the clear water. He and Jamie began to row the boat out onto the lake. He screamed in his head for them to stop, but it was useless.

The island drifted closer.

Jamie smiled and laughed as they rowed onward, occasionally looking back over his shoulder at it.

Jamie, please... Mark begged, wanting to sob, even though his present body showed no such capacity, *stop it.*

The smile on Jamie's face faded. He stared at Mark with a completely expressionless look. He dropped his oar and his arms fell by his sides.

Something felt like it had suddenly changed, like a bad omen moving over the water.

His head pointed downward. Mark stared at his odd figure and knew that he was seeing a side of his son that he'd never seen before—a side of his son that he never wanted to see.

With a sickening quickness, Jamie's head snapped up. There was a look in his eyes that no five-year-old should ever show: it was pure rage. A great and terrible rage, unexplained and without warning. He opened his mouth wide, brandishing his teeth.

The last image that Mark saw was Jamie's nightmarish face, inches from his own, twisted by a terrible force.

He opened his eyes and stared at the ceiling of his room, the morning sunlight pouring through the window.

— CHAPTER SEVEN —

Hunter, Cleaver and Firebug

By the time he got out of bed, the events of the night before were all a distant blur. He remembered the nightmare he had about Jamie attacking him in the boat, but he couldn't remember if everything else that happened in the night was part of the same dream.

He took a quick shower and got dressed, then left his room. Bright sunlight splashed across everything in the lounge. Pete wasn't anywhere to be seen, and he was thankful for that. In fact, there didn't seem to be anyone around. Only the sound of the ticking clock broke the silence.

His mind went to the sound of the clock when he crept around in the darkness the night before, chasing ghosts.

He made his way into the dining room to find a fresh pot of coffee sitting on the table. He sat down and poured himself some. The smell of it was quite good. He figured everything must have more of an authentic flavor out in the country.

His mug wasn't more than a quarter-emptied before the doors in the lounge swung open and someone walked in. It was Pete. He walked into the dining room, adjusting his hat. It wasn't until he sat down that he actually noticed Mark.

They looked at each other like deer caught in the headlights, neither of them knowing what to do. Mark broke the stalemate by sipping on his coffee.

Pete sat in awkward silence. He thought about pouring himself a cup, but he looked like he was struggling with the idea. Every few seconds he would glance over his shoulder at the doors, wondering if he should just get up and leave.

His hand was wrapped in medical dressings, a slight spot of red visible. A heavy feeling washed over Mark, making him feel guilty for what happened the night before. He thought for a moment, then opened his mouth to apologize to Pete.

The batwing doors suddenly opened and Felix came in, munching on a piece of toast. "Morning, guys," he said. "How is it?" he asked, nodding at Pete's bandaged hand.

Pete held it up and appraised it. "Not too bad. Doctor put five stitches in me. As long as it don't stop me from fishin'." He glanced at Mark with a flash of something condemning in his eyes.

Mark suddenly wished he hadn't crawled out of bed this morning.

"Let me fix you guys some breakfast," Felix said, turning to leave.

Pete stood up. "I'll grab some on my way out. I'm gonna tackle the lake... see what the rain dredged up for me."

Felix nodded. "You hungry, Mark?"

"Yeah, please." Mark tried not to look at Pete as he headed outside.

Felix went into the kitchen. The sounds of dishes clanging and refrigerators opening and closing punctuated the silence as Mark drank his coffee.

Two cups later, Felix came out holding two plates filled with eggs, bacon, hash browns and toast. The two of them dug in, spending the first few minutes in serene quiet.

Felix spoke up. "Don't feel too bad."

"Hmm?"

"For Pete," he said, nodding toward the lake.

Mark glanced out the window and saw Pete in a fishing boat sitting in the middle of the lake. He had his fishing pole propped under one arm as he struggled, trying to bait the line with his good hand.

"Oh," Mark said.

"He's had worse," Felix assured him.

"Big mean guy like that? I'll bet."

Felix laughed and started in on his toast.

Mark suddenly remembered what he saw out his window the night before. He was still half-trying to convince himself that it was just part of his dream, but there was something that felt too vivid about it in his memory.

"I noticed that island out on the lake," he said. "Is that part of the grounds here?"

Felix gave a bitter look, like it was a subject he didn't enjoy talking about. "One thing I forgot to mention," he said. "Don't go to that island. You want to take a fishing boat out and catch some bass, you go for it, but the island's off limits." He continued making an odd face, as if to say that he had nothing more to say on the subject.

"Someone was on that island last night."

"What?" Felix's eyes went wide. "What do you mean?"

"Just before I went to bed, I looked out the window in my room and saw someone standing on the shore of the island."

"What were they doing?"

"I don't know. It looked like they were taking something out of their boat, then they disappeared up a hill."

"What time did you say this was?"

"Just about midnight, I think."

Felix paused for a long time, deep in thought. Finally, he gave Mark a cursory glance and said: "Thanks for letting me know."

"What's the deal with that place, anyway?" Mark asked.

Felix let out a defeated sigh. "I couldn't even tell you if I wanted to. There's just something *wrong* with that place. All the locals around here know to stay away from it. The trees don't grow right, the wind seems to curve around it... Hell, even the wildlife doesn't go near that place."

A tingling sensation crawled up Mark's spine. The frightening imagery from his dream when he stood in front of the cabin came back to him.

"Is there anything on the island?" he asked, already expecting the answer. "Why would someone go there?"

"Beats me. Nothing there but an old cabin."

His heart skipped a beat. He was right. He *knew* it was there. But how? He'd never been anywhere near this lodge before.

"What's in that cabin?" he asked, leaning forward.

Felix shifted uncomfortably in his chair. "I'm telling you, Hector's the man to ask on that one. I'll say that there's a lot of history there, only some of it I know. But Hector knows all about it, as far as I can tell. He's been living on this lake for longer than I have, after all."

Mark was struck with a sudden thought: "Do you think it could have been Hector on the island last night?"

Felix let out a loud laugh that made Mark jump. "Hector? On the island? Hey, you want to see something funny, just try putting Hector in a boat. That man is absolutely *terrified* of water."

"Oh." Mark thought for a moment, then finished up the last of his hash browns.

Felix stood up and took their empty plates into the kitchen. Mark poured himself another cup of coffee, surprised by how much he enjoyed it. Felix returned, picking food out of his teeth with a toothpick.

"There was something else," Mark said. "When I was looking out my window last night, I also saw a man standing in the woods, looking at me."

"Where?" Felix sounded concerned.

"Up in the woods on the left side there," Mark replied, pointing.

Felix glanced down at the emptying pot of coffee with a morose look. "Was he a tall man?"

Mark was taken aback. "Yes! You know him?"

Felix gave a sarcastic laugh. "That man defines me. Him and his brothers." When Mark just looked at him in confused silence, he continued. "Remember when I told you last night about that case I was so obsessed over?"

Mark nodded.

"That was them," Felix said. "The tall one that you saw goes by the name of Hunter. Well, that's what everybody calls him, anyway. The middle brother of the family we call Cleaver. And the youngest one is Firebug."

"Firebug?"

"Just as the name implies."

"Who are they?"

"If you ask anyone else, they're just a few creepy loners who live off the land in the woods. If you ask me, they're serial killers."

Mark's coffee mug slipped out of his fingers, bouncing off the table and spilling all over it.

"Ah shit, sorry," Mark said, getting up.

"They usually have that effect on people," Felix said with a smile.

Mark grabbed a dish towel sitting just inside the kitchen and cleaned up the mess.

"Those three have always been a mysterious bunch," Felix continued. "They live up in that dilapidated house on the hill. It's an old, old house. Been there for over a century. Nobody knows exactly when, but somewhere along the line those three moved into town. They've never spoken a word to anyone. Some people think they're mute."

"Do they ever come into town?"

"They've been in town a couple of times over the years. Scares the holy shit out of anyone who walks by them." Felix noted Mark's inquisitive look. "If you saw them up close, you'd understand. Real scary-looking bunch, like they just escaped off the prison bus. They're always dressed in these shabby rags. Probably haven't washed them in years."

"So Firebug is an arsonist, then?" Mark asked.

Felix nodded. "Their nicknames were actually given to them innocently enough, but they're also pretty representative of who they really are, too."

"Which are serial killers?"

"That's right. Not long after I became sheriff, people noticed these boys in town. The last owner of this lodge told everyone that he saw them up in the woods, living in that house. He's the one who coined the names."

"How'd he pick them?" Mark asked.

"Well, the owner always saw the tall one hunting animals out in the woods, so he called him Hunter. Cleaver always chops the wood for their fires. Him and his axe are inseparable. The youngest one always starts the fires, always playing around with his lighter; so, Firebug."

"And these guys have been murdering people?"

"That's what I kept trying to tell everyone, but no one would listen to me. About a year after I became sheriff, people started turning up dead in gruesome ways around town. Some folks had been disappearing, too."

"Was there ever any proof it was them?"

"There was some," Felix said, "but it was only circumstantial. These guys were smarter than everyone pegged them for."

"So how'd you know?"

"The murders started happening just after these guys turned up in town. Each of the victims died in one of three ways. I worked out an MO for each brother, based on the little that we've seen of them. And wouldn't you know it, the nicknames we gave them are pretty telling of how each of them kills."

Felix leaned in, his voice becoming hushed. "Firebug usually kills whole families at a time. He'll set fire to their house at night when everyone's sleeping and barricade all the doors. He douses the entire perimeter of their house with kerosene and creates a ring of fire all around. By the time the family realizes what's going on, it's usually too late."

Mark's stomach churned. "And the other two?"

"There've never been any survivors of the two oldest brothers." Felix shrugged. "None that we know about, anyway.

"A few months after the fires started," he continued, "we got a string of murders where the victims were, uh... well, let's just say there was an axe involved."

"And you live right down the hill from these psychos?" Mark asked in disbelief.

A coy look came over Felix's face. "Well, call me crazy—my wife certainly did—but..." He thought about his words. "I did it to keep a closer eye on them. Back when I was still sheriff, I started to piece things together and realized that these three freaks were the killers. But someone taught them how to cover their tracks, because we could never get any solid evidence on them."

"Did you ever question them?"

Felix chuckled. "We tried, a few times. But trying to question a mute who has no concept of social interaction doesn't go too far. It was always a big waste of time."

"What about their house? Didn't you search it?"

"We did," Felix said. "Well... we tried to, anyway. When I finally got a search warrant, I even got the support of six officers from the big town over, Langdale. They came with me and my deputy to the house, but when we got there the brothers weren't home. So we broke the door in and I went in first. Unfortunately for me," he said, patting his knee, "the doorway was booby-trapped. They rigged a blade to swing when someone tripped a wire. The blade cut deep into my knee and shattered some of the bone. Took a few operations before I was able to walk again."

"Did anyone else go in?"

"*No one* was going in after that," Felix said. "Who knows what else could have been in there. The paramedics came and took me to the hospital. I wasn't there for the rest, but my deputy told me about the homecoming they gave those brothers."

Mark leaned forward so much that the edge of the table cut into his stomach. "What did they do?"

"The other officers waited until the brothers got home to arrest them," Felix said, "but when they arrived and saw their front door broken down, they went apeshit."

Mark's eyes widened at the thought. "And?"

"Firebug attacked first. He beat on an officer pretty bad. Cleaver joined in, but a couple of the other officers restrained him before he did much damage. Hunter made the mistake of pulling a knife. They put seven shots into him before he finally hit the ground."

"*Seven?* And he *lived?*"

"He healed pretty quick, too. The three of them stood trial. Well... if you can call it that; they just sat there in silence for the whole thing while their lawyer did the talking. It's not like they could testify or anything. The judge sentenced each of them, and they all did time over in Langdale."

"How long?"

"Not enough. Firebug got five years, Cleaver got three, and Hunter got fourteen for pulling the knife. The boys over in Langdale called it a slam dunk, but they just didn't get it. The brothers need to be put away for life. Actually, the electric chair would be better on my nerves, knowing they're gone for good."

"Did the murders stop when they were in jail?" Mark asked.

"Well, the murders had kind of dried up for a while before they went to jail," Felix said. "The last one that I know of happened in West Union. After a while, they got a little bit wiser and started going to different towns to kill. Eventually the murders petered out for the most part and the disappearances started happening."

"They started kidnapping their victims instead?"

"Seems that way," Felix said.

"What for?"

"Probably to kill them more discreetly, but I can't say for sure."

"So did the disappearances stop when they were in jail?" Mark pressed.

"That's the problem," Felix said. "They didn't."

Mark looked disbelievingly at Felix. "Was it really them, then?"

"It was. I *know* it was." An almost pleading look came over Felix's face. "There must have been someone else at play. That's something I never figured out, though."

"So you bought this lodge to keep an eye on them when they got out of prison?" Mark asked.

"Yeah," Felix said, feeling guilty. "My wife and I got into a huge argument about it. I tried explaining that it was for the good of a lot of innocent lives, but she already stopped listening to me a long time before that. We got divorced and she got custody of Stephanie. They moved down to Florida and I never saw them again. After it happened, I tried reasoning with myself that I was doing what I had to by buying this place, but the only person I was fooling was me. The disappearances eventually died down. The brothers have been keeping pretty quiet for a long time. I was so caught up in my obsession for all these years, and now when I look at myself in the mirror, all I see is a tired old man."

Mark let out a sharp breath. It was a lot of information to take in. Overwhelming, really. His stomach tied itself in knots wondering if one of these three cretins had killed his family while he was at work. But he couldn't understand why. He needed more information.

"You never did tell me how Hunter kills people," he said.

"He breaks into a person's house and covers all their windows so the light doesn't get in. Then when the victim comes home, he cuts all the power to their house. As the victim stumbles around in the dark, he hunts them. It's like a sick sport to him."

"Wouldn't he be stumbling around in the dark, too?" Mark asked.

"You would think so, but I don't think that's the case. My theory is that he has a photographic memory and a good sense of space. I think he surveys the house before the victim comes home and commits it all to memory. The only thing we've seen from the victim's blood is that Hunter plays with them for a while. There always looks to be a struggle in front of doors or windows; I think that whenever the victim tries to escape, Hunter tosses them back into the house. The way he always finishes is by gutting the victim. Drags his knife up their stomach just like an animal. Makes me sick every time. But like the others, he's never left any evidence behind that it was him."

A slow and creeping horror dawned on Mark. "Who did you say the man I saw in the woods was?"

"Well, if he was really tall, like you said, it must have been Hunter," Felix replied, not sure where Mark was going with this.

"He was here last night," Mark said in a frightened tone.

Felix went pale. After a few seconds struggling to speak, he finally croaked out: "*What?*"

"When I saw him out in the woods, I looked away for a second, then when I looked back, he was gone. I couldn't find him anywhere, and a few seconds later, I heard the door to the lodge opening."

"Which door?" Felix asked, his eyes narrowing.

"One of those doors leading into the lounge," Mark said, pointing.

"Are you *sure* it was the door?"

"Well, I think it was. But it was late at night, maybe I was imagining things."

"What happened next?" Felix pressed.

"I was just kind of stunned in my room. I started hearing sounds like someone was walking across the floor. They stopped on the other side of my door, and then I'm not really sure, but it sounded like someone was scratching on it. And when I opened it, there was no one there. I searched the lounge but didn't see anyone."

"So what did you do?" Felix asked.

"I went to bed. I thought it was my imagination, but now I'm not so sure."

Felix rested his chin on his hands and stared at the wall in front of him. "What would he want with me?" he asked, mostly to himself. "They leave me alone for all these years... why now?"

Mark interjected. "Do you think it has something to do with me?"

Felix dismissed the thought.

"Don't forget," Mark said, "someone wanted me to come to this lodge. They might be the ones. Felix... do you think one of them... was at my house two days ago?" Tears stung his eyes as he said the words.

"You said your family was killed in the daytime while you were at work?" Felix asked.

"Yes."

"Then it wasn't Hunter; he only kills at night. Cleaver's been known to kill in the daytime before, but unless your family was chopped up into little pieces, then it wasn't him." Felix froze, suddenly horrified at what he just said. "They weren't... were they?"

"No," Mark said.

"Sorry Mark, but I don't think the brothers had anything to do with what happened to your family. Like I said, your best bet is to talk to Hector."

"Right," Mark said. "I think I'll go do that."

They gave each other a nod and Felix got up and left. Mark stood up and looked out the window. Pete was still sitting in his boat. He was in the middle of reeling in a fish when the line snapped and he fell back on his butt. Then he pounded his good hand on the side of the boat, mouthing a torrent of what Mark assumed were swear words. Mark couldn't help but laugh. He turned and walked to the lounge doors, ready to head off to Hector's cottage.

"Mark!" Felix yelled from somewhere in the lodge.

He spun around and ran toward his room down the hall. Felix was standing in front of it, staring at the door.

There was an odd symbol carved into the front of it. It looked like two vertical lines, each with two short diagonal lines crossed through it.

"I... I didn't see it... this morning," Mark stammered.

They stood in stunned silence. Mark looked past Felix and saw something even more terrifying in his room. He pushed past him and picked up his family's portrait sitting on the writing desk.

The faces of everyone in the picture had red 'X's drawn over them.

— CHAPTER EIGHT —

THE BLACK WARDEN

The sun stayed out into the early afternoon, casting a hot and sticky net over the grassy hills and gravel pathways. Mark skirted along the path edging the lake that led up toward Hector's cottage. The faces of his family crossed out in red ink floated through his mind over and over again. As he walked, he occasionally shot a glance over his shoulder at the brothers' house sitting deep in the woods. Looking at it in the daylight now, he could see a disturbing detail: all the windows of the house were boarded up. He wondered if they did it to keep people from seeing what was really inside. Felix didn't think the brothers had anything to do with his family's deaths, but the fact that Hunter crossed off the faces of his family was a little too strong to ignore. He hoped his meeting with Hector would shed some light on these increasingly dark mysteries.

When he started to climb up the hill that Hector's cottage stood on, the sound of a truck's engine echoed from behind. He turned around and saw a beige pickup truck pull to a stop in front of the brothers' house up in the woods. The engine cut out and three thin, lanky men climbed out of the cab. Hunter was instantly recognizable to Mark; his sheer size compared to the other two was unmistakable. The three of them went up to the house. One of the shorter ones had long, greasy hair and wore a tattered blue shirt; the other one was a little gaunter, and there was something abnormal about the way he walked. Mark wondered which was Cleaver and which was Firebug until the brother in the blue shirt with the long hair took a detour to the side of the house and picked up an axe that leaned against it. He inspected the blade for a moment, then wiped it against his shirt, as if he was cleaning something off of it. A moment later, Cleaver turned and rejoined his brothers as the three of them disappeared into the house. Mark looked at the house for a moment longer as an uneasy feeling rose up in the pit of his stomach. He turned back around and continued up toward Hector's.

He crested the hill and came to the peaceful and quaint cottage that seemed to shimmer in the summer's light. As he rounded a corner, looking for the front door, he found Hector bent over a garden.

"Hello, Hector."

Hector dropped his trowel and shot up like a volt of electricity coursed through his spine.

"Oh! It's you, my boy," he said, letting out a relieved sigh. "You startled me."

"Sorry about that," Mark said, offering a smile.

A HAUNTING AT HOLLOW'S COVE

Hector took off his gloves and wiped his hands down his gardening shirt. "So what brings you here today?"

Mark leaned against the side of the house, which offered a thin reprieve from the sun's harsh light. "Felix mentioned that you knew a lot about the lodge and this general area."

"I should hope so," Hector said, adjusting his straw hat. "I've been living here for the past seventy years, give or take." He patted Mark on the shoulder. "Come on inside. It's boiling out here."

The two of them walked to the porch and went through the front door. The cottage was much bigger than it looked from the outside, offering Mark a splendid view of tasteful rugs and furnishings as they came into the living room. A large fireplace sat in the far wall, though it was left ignored in the summers, and a sunroom sat behind it with an entrance on either side. Immediately to Mark's right was a closed door secured with a padlock. The kitchen was next to it, and on the other side of the living room was a hallway that led to bedrooms and a bathroom.

Hector gestured for Mark to take a seat in a big armchair and Mark sank into the plump maroon leather upholstery. Hector disappeared into the kitchen for a moment and returned displaying a bottle of wine.

"Would you care for a drink?" he asked.

"Isn't it a little early for alcohol?" Mark said, trying to figure out if Hector was joking or not.

Hector shrugged. "I always like to extend the courtesy," he said with a friendly smile.

Mark gave a short laugh. "Thank you, but I don't drink."

Hector looked genuinely disappointed. "Oh... why is that?"

"Bad history of alcoholism in the family," Mark said, feeling slightly uncomfortable.

"That's a terrible shame. You have my sympathies." Hector disappeared around the corner into the kitchen and came back empty-handed. He joined Mark in the living room and sat in an armchair across from him. He took off his straw hat and set it on the floor next to his chair, running a hand through his sweaty hair. "So, my dear boy," he said, "what would you like to talk about?"

"Well," Mark said, hesitant, "I guess I should start off with why I'm here." He paused. "The lodge, I mean."

Hector nodded, attentively awaiting what he had to say.

"Two days ago, I came home from work, and... I... my family was inside." Mark felt uncomfortable trying to explain something so grisly. Hector shared none of his discomfort, looking like a person who was waiting to hear what the weather was going to be for the next week. "They were dead."

Hector's smile slid down his face. "*Dead?*"

Mark looked down at his shoes. "Murdered."

"What happened?"

"I don't know. That's why I'm here; I was kind of hoping you could help me out." He reached into his back pocket and pulled out the Hollow's Cove brochure, handing it to him.

Hector's eyes danced rapidly over the cover.

"I found this on my doorstep that morning," Mark said. "Someone sent it to me."

"I don't understand," Hector said, flipping open the cover and revealing the spread inside. "Do you think this had something to—" He stared at the brochure with wide eyes.

Mark leaned forward in his chair. "Do you know what it means?"

Hector didn't say a word; he only stared as if the most dreadful thing he'd ever seen sat in front of him. After a moment, he rubbed a hand across his chin and sat quietly in consideration.

"Well?" Mark said, eager that he seemed to know something.

But still Hector didn't speak. He stood up and walked over to a window overlooking the lake.

A terrible feeling knotted Mark's stomach when he slowly realized that Hector was looking at the island. Then it *was* connected. There was some kind of tie between what happened to his family and that dreadful island.

"*Well?*" Mark repeated. The word came out sharply and seemed to startle both of them. "Who is the Black Warden? What does that mean?"

Hector snapped out of his trance and returned to his armchair. He seemed unfazed by Mark's impatience, his eyes dreamily staring down at the brochure. He slowly surfaced into reality again and collected his thoughts. "The Black Warden is a nickname," he said. "A moniker for a man you don't ever want to meet. His real name was Nathaniel Fischer, and he was the man who built this lodge."

"When was this?" Mark asked.

"He bought the land and began construction in 1890."

"1890?" Mark repeated incredulously. "How could a man who was alive in 1890 want something to do with me? Isn't he dead?"

"That's the problem," Hector said. "The fact that his return is being threatened is worrying, to say the least."

"But dead people can't come back to life!" Mark protested. As soon as he'd said it, his son Jamie immediately came to mind. "Can they?"

"I don't know," Hector admitted. "It's possible."

"It's possible? Just who the hell was this guy?"

"He started out as a man," Hector replied, "just like you or me. He had a wife and four daughters. He was of the entrepreneurial spirit and began constructing the lodge. It was meant to be a vacation spot, much like it is now, but it was supposed to be much bigger. The other parts of the campgrounds were to be built upon after the lodge was complete. But Nathaniel was interrupted midway through the project."

"By what?"

"By that island," Hector said, nodding his head toward the window.

Mark looked over at the ominous patch of land floating on the water.

"He discovered something on that island that he could never forget. Something... captivating."

"Does it have something to do with a cabin in the middle of it?"

Hector cast a suspicious look. "How did you know there was a cabin there?"

"I don't know," Mark said. "I've been having these awful dreams lately, and I saw that cabin. I don't know how I know, but I know something terrible happened in there."

"That doesn't even begin to describe it, I'm afraid," Hector said with a frown. "Before the cabin was built there, it was just an empty island, completely devoid of all life. It's like a floating marvel. Nothing of its kind has ever been told of before, and no one dares to go near it. But Nathaniel was drawn to its strange power."

"Power?" Mark sputtered.

"There's something that lives at the heart of that island; a presence. It's intangible; it has no color, no sound, no feeling, no smell. But it's very real."

"What kind of presence are we talking about here?"

"Well," Hector said, considering, "it's evil itself. I don't think there's a better way to describe it. By itself, it does nothing. But nothing living can go near it. All of the trees grow in odd shapes, and no animals have ever been spotted on the island. Birds don't even fly over it. They just know that there's something *wrong* there. Unfortunately, men don't have the keen instincts of animals, and many men have found nothing but insanity and death on that island.

"When someone comes in contact with the presence, their mind becomes subject to its influence. The deeper into the island they go, the stronger the evil becomes. And what they begin to find is their mind slipping. They start to conjure images in their head that aren't necessarily so. In the beginning, it's akin to becoming a violent drunk. But as the evil's influence creeps further and further into a person's psyche, it creates more of a crazed maniac. Some people's minds are stronger and able to withstand the force better than others. Some people are extremely susceptible to it; for these people, they go past murderous lunatic over time and their mind simply degrades into disuse."

"Was Nathaniel resistant to it?" Mark asked.

"Not entirely. He was able to stave off its harsher effects, but nonetheless the evil pulled him into its influence. But it didn't quite have the same effect on him as it did the others; where others were pushed to violence, Nathaniel was simply captivated and eventually fell into obsession.

"His own pursuit of power caused him to create a connection with the island's presence. He wanted to know more about it, to study it. Just as construction on the main lodge completed, he halted production on the campgrounds' other facilities and made the workers build him a cabin at the center of the island where the presence was strongest. He wanted to have a command center, so to speak, to experiment and study the evil. Of course, the workers were entirely susceptible to the pervading evil as well, and it didn't take long before they became aggressive. Heated arguments turned into fistfights, which turned into bloodshed. Nathaniel began to conduct social experiments on the workers. Things became too perverse for me to say from there."

"Why didn't the workers leave?" Mark asked.

"Some tried. But their minds were too weakened to do much. Nathaniel spirited away with the unruly ones."

"What did he do to them?" Mark asked, his heart feeling heavier and heavier.

"Apparently he did, um... some surgical experiments on them. When his cabin was finished, he took all of them for his experiments. They were all foreign laborers, so no one went looking for them."

Mark's stomach sank to the floor. "That's insane," he said. "This is all one big joke, right?"

Hector shook his head. "I'm very serious. Everything I'm telling you was detailed by Nathaniel himself in his old journals. I've collected police reports over the years that corroborate everything I'm saying."

"You have his journals?" Mark asked.

"Yes. He stored them in a secret place in the lodge. When the owner of the lodge before Felix found them, he offered them to me, knowing how much of a history buff I was. At first they seemed innocent enough, but their insidious nature soon became apparent. I very much wish I could go back to that day and decline the journals."

"So where was Nathaniel's family the entire time he was doing those things?"

"His wife and four daughters were staying at the lodge the entire time," Hector said. "He kept them in the dark as to what he was doing when he was gone all day and night. But they became increasingly aware of the fact that they were in the presence of someone very dangerous. Finally, one day, Nathaniel's wife decided to sneak out with their daughters and leave."

"Did they make it?"

"Well, by this point, the police had caught wind of what was going on. They went to the lodge to investigate, and upon their arrival, they found large amounts of blood spilt inside."

"He killed them?" Mark asked.

"Supposedly, but their bodies were never found," Hector replied. "Neither was Nathaniel. All of them simply disappeared."

"Was he ever heard from again?"

"No," Hector said in a grim tone. "Near the end, he began referencing a tomb that he built for himself in one of his journals. He talked about laying himself to rest."

"Surely he's dead," Mark said, more to himself than to Hector. "All of that happened over a hundred years ago."

"That's what I thought, too," Hector said. "But after seeing that brochure, and what you've told me of your family, I'm not so certain anymore."

"There was something else," Mark said.

"Hmm?"

He pulled out a piece of paper from his pocket and handed it to Hector. "Have you ever seen it before?" he asked.

Hector studied it and slowly shook his head. "It doesn't ring a bell. What is it?"

"That symbol was carved on my door in the lodge last night by Hunter. You're familiar with the brothers, right?"

Hector swallowed hard. "Yes. They're a very unsavory bunch, but Felix knows more about them than I do. And... you said that he was *inside* the lodge?"

"Yeah, I saw him standing in the woods last night, then I heard noises, like someone was coming inside and then this weird scratching on my door... I thought I was just hearing things, but when I woke up this morning, that symbol was carved into it and he crossed off the faces of my family on the picture I brought. Hector, do you think they're working for Nathaniel?"

"I don't know. It's possible they could have found a way to resurrect him. It must sound crazy to you, but you don't even know the half of what Nathaniel achieved with the power he found on that island. He described doing things that the laws of science can't even account for."

Mark nodded slowly as he thought about this. "Hector, there's one more thing... When I found my family, I heard someone else in the house with me. I snuck around, thinking I would see the killer, but it wasn't. It was my son."

"He wasn't killed?" Hector asked.

"That's the thing... he was. But he was also standing in front of me—I swear he was—but he was like a ghost. Does that make any sense?"

"No, it doesn't," Hector said.

Mark's heart sank. After a moment, he added, "Do you think Nathaniel killed my family?"

"I don't know," Hector admitted. "It sounds like him, but I don't know how that's possible."

"So what should I do?"

Hector thought for a moment. He stood up and disappeared down the hallway, returning a few minutes later with a small stack of books.

"The journals?" Mark asked.

"Mhmm." He dropped them in Mark's lap. "Read through them if you like. See if there's anything there that might give you an idea. I have a few more myself that I'll search. Hopefully something will jog my memory."

"What's this?" Mark asked, seeing a photo poking out between two of the journals. He pulled it out and studied it. It showed a tall and vigorous-looking young man, maybe in his mid-to-late twenties, with short, dark hair. The photo was black and white, and the suit that the man wore denoted the age of the picture as well. Studying his face, Mark saw sharp cheeks, fire in his eyes and, though he was smiling, a stern and overbearing presence to the man. Something almost evil.

"Is this?" he asked.

"Yes," Hector replied. "The Black Warden."

— CHAPTER NINE —

Last Call

By the time Mark got back to the lodge, his head was spinning with dizzying images and scenarios. The thought of a man he didn't know and supposedly long-dead hunting him was terrifying, to say the least. He couldn't think of a reason why someone would kill his family, or why they wanted him to come here; it just didn't make any sense.

Evening set in and a hint of orange began to stretch across the sky. Mark had glanced through bits of the first journal Hector gave him on his walk back to the lodge. He couldn't make much sense of them, but he would pore over them later when he could clear his head.

The lodge was quiet as he walked into the lounge. Pete was nowhere in sight, and Mark supposed he had finally taken his breakfast and left for the day. He wondered if he might show up later that night and felt himself apprehensive at the idea.

He stashed the journals in his room and came out to talk to Felix, who was tidying up in the main entrance. Felix fixed them some dinner, and as they ate Mark told him what Hector had said. He didn't think he'd ever seen Felix spend such a long, continuous amount of time forgetting to blink. In the end, Felix didn't say much, simply because he was at a loss for words.

As the evening crept toward night, Jerry showed up. The three of them sat in the lounge talking for a while, and for Mark, things were about as comfortable as they could get at the moment.

"Mark!" Felix suddenly cried. "I forgot to show you..." He reached into his shirt pocket and pulled out something glittering. He held out his hand.

Mark leaned forward and looked at the object. It was a golden locket in the shape of a T-rex. He slowly took it out of Felix's hand and opened it. Inside was a picture of Felix, his face beaming.

"So, what do you think?" Felix asked eagerly.

"I'm flattered, Felix," Mark replied, his face contorted in confusion. "You shouldn't have."

"Very funny," Felix said. "It's for my grandson, Jacob."

"Oh," Mark said, handing the locket back.

"Stephanie tells me Jacob loves dinosaurs, so I thought I'd get him this for his birthday to remind him of me between visits. I also bought him a new bike, but I hope he really likes this, too. It's the meaningful gifts that you really remember, you know?"

"He'll love it," Mark said.

"It looks great," Jerry chimed in, leaning over to inspect it. "I'm sure he'll get a kick out of it. How old is Jacob going to be?"

"Six," Felix said.

"You know, it's very good that Jacob is going to get to grow up with his grandpa," Jerry said. "Both of my grandpas died when I was young, and I never had that kind of person in my life. He's a lucky boy."

Felix smiled. "I sure hope so. I hope he likes me. I mean, I've never met him before, so it could go either way. It might not be that fun for him when the crazy old coot crashes his birthday party."

"I'm sure he'll like you just fine," Mark said.

Felix gave him a thin smile that quickly faded.

A door in the main entrance to the lodge opened and heavy footsteps came down the hall. Pete came around the corner and sat down on the empty stool next to Mark. A tightness gripped Mark as he tried to glance over at his injured hand without being obvious. He knew it was just a matter of time before Pete came back, but that didn't make the situation any less awkward.

Jerry leaned over. "Nice to see you, Pete!"

"How you doing, Pete?" Felix asked.

"None too bad, Felix, none too bad," Pete said. "I've got this wild cramp in my hand that just won't seem to go away, though." He held up his injured hand and pretended to study it for a moment.

Felix watched Pete carefully. "Beer?" he asked.

"What else would it be?"

Mark drummed his fingers on the bar, wishing he had something to keep them busy.

"I'll take a beer."

Felix spun around as if someone had just slapped him. "What was that?" he asked.

"I said I'll have a beer," Mark said.

Felix stared at him for a moment, chewing a toothpick, then pulled another one out of the fridge.

"Don't be too surprised, there, Felix," Pete said. "He probably just wants his turn to get drunk and come at me with a bottle." Pete slapped his good hand down on Mark's shoulder. "Figure 'bout one beer'll do him till he's wobblin' all over the place, isn't that right, Mark?"

Mark ignored him and started drinking his beer. He didn't like the taste, but he forced himself to keep drinking. He'd never had this feeling before, but he felt like he *needed* a drink. He always stayed away from it because he didn't want to turn into his father, but he had failed miserably at protecting his family anyway, so what did it matter now?

"Goes down smooth, doesn't it?" Pete said.

Mark gave him a passive nod.

"Forgettin' about the ol' wife yet?" Pete asked. "Ah, don't worry, Mark, it gets easier once you realize she was a stinkin' bitch."

Mark paused, the tip of the bottle balancing on his lips. A red-hot swell of hatred flooded inside of him, but he fought against it and waited until it passed before continuing on his beer.

"Just pawn that ring and get it over with," Pete continued. "That's what I did after my first wife. Plus it'll free her up for a real man like me."

Mark shot him a scathing look. His hand tightened on the bottle. "*Drop* it, Pete."

"Look buddy, all I'm sayin' is ol' Pete knows how to show a woman a good time. Cryin' your little tears ain't gonna change that." He slid a napkin across the bar top to Mark. "So why don't you write that little minx's number down for me."

Mark stood up and raised his beer bottle, enraged and on the verge of smashing it against the bar. Waves of amber beer and foam rushed out of it and splashed on the floor.

"Mark!" Felix barked.

Pete stood up too, squarely facing him and puffing his chest out. "Do it," he said, loosening his arms up by his sides. "I've been waiting."

Mark held the bottle over the bar, suspended for what seemed like forever, everyone's eyes focused on it. It took everything he had not to do it. Finally, he lowered it and put it down on the bar. "My wife is dead!" he bellowed.

The room went completely silent. Pete's chest deflated and he slumped back down onto his barstool. He opened his mouth and fumbled for words, finally ending up with a quiet "What?"

Mark instantly felt his temper drain away. He rubbed his temples and expelled a sharp breath. "My wife was murdered two days ago. My children, too."

"Oh my God," Jerry whispered to himself.

Pete was still dumbstruck. After a few moments to process what was said, he leaned forward on the bar and buried his face in his hands. Then he raised his head and looked at Mark, completely changed. "I'm so sorry," he said with sincerity. "I had no idea."

"No, you didn't," Mark said.

"No, really," Pete pressed, "I mean it. My wife's mother was murdered by a home intruder six years ago."

"She was?"

"Yeah. It's gotta be the hardest thing you could ever go through. Listen, I'm real sorry about everything I said. I was just tryin' to get a rise outta ya. I didn't know you were goin' through all this."

Mark stared at Pete for a while before he said: "It's okay. Let's just forget about it."

Pete nodded.

Felix finally remembered to start breathing again, and his chest rose and fell in large heaves. For one horrifying second, he thought he had swallowed his toothpick and not noticed, but then remembered he was holding it in his fingers.

"Listen Mark," Jerry said, "if you ever need anything, we're all friends here."

"Thanks," Mark said.

Pete stood up. "Well, let's get this place a little more lively!" He walked over and turned on the jukebox. It whirred into life and the energetic sounds of "China Grove" by the Doobie Brothers came on. Ten seconds into the song, the lights on the jukebox began to waver then it shut off.

"Ah come on, Felix, you really gotta get this fixed!" Pete said.

"I'll call a guy next week, I promise," Felix replied.

Pete stormed off and disappeared down the guest-rooms hallway, stomping down a flight of stairs.

"The wiring for that breaker is a little screwy," Felix explained to Mark.

A moment later, the jukebox came back to life and Pete returned. He sat back down and nursed his beer, gently swaying his head to the music.

For the rest of the night, all four of them had a good time. Pete was nothing but friendly to Mark and Mark was glad for it. Near the end of his beer, Mark started to enjoy it and drank another one. The journals weighed heavily on his mind and there was an itch inside of him that wanted to rush off and grab them, but he needed to soothe his nerves first. The image of Nathaniel flashed behind his eyes and he shuddered.

"Everything all right, Mark?" Felix asked, resting a hand on his shoulder.

"Yeah, everything's fine." He stared blankly at the wall ahead and sipped his beer.

— CHAPTER TEN —

Following the Paper Trail

Pete and Jerry left shortly after eleven o'clock, and Felix was on his way to bed.

"You turning in too, Mark?" Felix asked.

"No, I'm going to look over those journals in the library for a bit if you don't mind," Mark said.

"Not at all. Just make sure to turn the lights off when you're finished. Oh, and feel free to look at any other books in the library as well. Most of it is just general stuff that probably won't help you, but there are a few books about local events."

Mark nodded. "Thanks, I'll take a look."

Felix gave him a wave and went up the staircase to his room.

Mark grabbed the three journals from his room that Hector gave him. He paused at the window and looked out over the nighttime landscape. The island didn't look like there were any signs of activity; no boats shored up and no people dressed in black cloaks. He wondered if the person he saw the night before was somehow, against all odds, Nathaniel himself. He then wondered if the brothers really were trying to resurrect him. He shuddered at the thought. He glanced at the brothers' house then down into the woods. No sign of Hunter.

Letting out a nervous sigh, he took the journals and made his way to the library. It was about half the size of the lounge with a wide plate glass window overlooking the parking lot. Bookshelves took up both sides of the room, and there were two long tables sitting between them. Frosted lamps adorned the walls, giving off a warm glow. Mark sat at one of the tables and got to work.

He laid the photo of Nathaniel on the table and studied it, then he took a journal and read the first entry:

June 14th, 1890

Today is the first day of construction and I am very excited to witness what could be a landmark achievement not only in my life, but in the nearby community as well. Hollow's Cove will be a grand monument of rest and relaxation to the whole of South Carolina and its neighboring states.

We begin by digging where the foundation for the main lodge will be laid. As I write this entry now, I can hear the workers digging out in the field. I found myself so excited this morning that I could barely contain myself. In a week's time I will bring Rosemary and the girls along to witness the beginning of a wonderful new life.

Mark flipped through the pages, glancing quickly at the following entries. All of them chronicled Nathaniel's progress with the lodge's construction and his plans for expansions to the resort. But there didn't seem to be anything pertinent to Mark. He reached the end of the journal and set it aside, reaching over and taking the next one, a more worn one with a burgundy binding.

It took him until halfway through the second journal before he found something interesting:

October 9th, 1890

As I write this entry, I find myself unable to sufficiently concentrate on what needs to be transcribed. However, I press on and attempt to commit the details of my discovery to paper. I have a pounding headache that cannot seem to be quelled, and it is from that isolated spot of land on the lake.

Today I finally decided to take a rowboat out to the desolate island by myself and explore the unexplored. The reason I call the island desolate will be described in the following entry. For now, I must retire. I can no longer fight the undeniable urge to rest and clear my head.

Mark felt his heart race. He turned the page and read the next entry:

JEFF DEGORDICK

October 10th, 1890

When I awoke this morning, I came to the terrifying realization that the pounding in my head did not go away. It indeed has lessened, but remains in a strange form that almost feels like it is a part of me. In a way the dull pounding feels like it has always been a part of me. Rosemary fixed me a cup of lemon tea, but my ailment seemed to have sidestepped the remedy entirely. Regardless, I must tell of what I found on that island.

As I said before, it was desolate. I do not mean to say that it was completely barren; in fact, there was an abundant amount of trees and sparse underbrush here or there. It was the fact that all of it was dead. As far as I could tell, there seemed to be no life on that forsaken island whatsoever. As I walked through the woods, I felt a cold presence in the air that seemed to intensify the deeper I got. Consistent with the evident fact that the island holds no life, I get the impression that the area is cold because heat cannot penetrate its icy shell. It feels like a void. So far, the presence is a complete mystery to me.

Despite my pounding head, I feel a strange compulsion to return to the island. There is something alluring about that place.

Mark read on as Nathaniel recounted his personal discoveries of the island's bizarre presence, his decision to build a cabin at the center of it, and the strange effects that the presence had on the workers.

He felt frustrated. It was all information that Hector already told him. Of course, the journals went into more detail, but there was nothing useful that could give him an idea why Nathaniel or someone working for him might be after him and his family.

He thumbed through the last of the pages and stopped on the final entry, maintaining a faint amount of hope.

November 29th, 1890

The cabin's progress is becoming slower and slower due to the increased violence amongst the laborers. That aspect, in itself, is frustrating, but it carries the welcomed side effect of being able to study the strange effects this presence has on humans.

Yesterday, one of the workers broke another's back. The man fell to the ground where he lay helpless. I decided to leave him there in the midst of the others and see what becomes of him. I am eager to return today and discover if the workers really are as depraved as I believe they have become.

I have been administering my influence well on the workers. As hostile as they are becoming with each other, they seem to demonstrate no ill will toward me, even as I stand in their midst. In fact, I am quite sure I have seen the looks of anguish and fear every time one of them glances at me. As with all of the recent developments, there is of course the occasional worker that does not quite fear me as he should. In my consideration of the chaos today, I had not even noticed one of the more emaciated workers sneak up behind me, brandishing a blade. He managed two quick slices on my left arm just behind the bicep before I subdued him. As I returned to my quarters in the lodge here, just before writing this entry, I cleaned my wound. Once the blood and loose skin were removed, I noticed my wound was in the form of a large and rather neat 'X'-shape. This shall be my reminder that I still have work to do.

I have also been pondering what to do about the project's foreman. The presence seems to have an effect on his mind as well, but not to the degree of the others. Simply put, the presence is just not 'taking' with him. This may fall in line with an idea I have been considering for the past few weeks: I have been thinking of building a subterranean 'testing grounds', so to speak, off the main campgrounds. I have found the perfect location, too. I spied a plot hidden in the woods one mile due west of the lake. An old, overgrown spot that no one will go looking for or find. It will be large enough to facilitate all of my experiments while remaining hidden from the resort's patrons. As certain desirable guests present themselves, it will not be difficult to take them down to the area and experiment on them. In the meantime, I think I will hold the foreman in my custody until the testing grounds are built.

Mark shuddered. *Subterranean testing grounds?* he thought. *Did he actually build such a place? And if he did, where is it? One mile west of the lake is too vague.*

But despite this interesting find, it didn't change the fact that the entry didn't shed any more light on his problem. Mark became bitter and snapped the journal shut, tossing it aside on the table. He dropped his head into his hands and let out a long, tired sigh.

There must be something! he thought. He looked around at the shelves of books all around him. After all, the lodge and library did used to belong to Nathaniel.

He got up and pulled out books at random, checking their contents for an indication of the date they were written as well as for any noteworthy information. To his dismay, most of the books were written within the last five decades. Various subjects flashed before his eyes as he tipped each book out. As he got to the end of the first bookshelf, something caught his attention.

A thin, black book poked out from the bottom corner, covered in dust and wedged between two thicker books. There was nothing written on its spine. Mark pulled it out and found that its cover was blank. It was so nondescript that he was about to put it back, but it struck him as odd, too; every other book in the library was clearly marked and covered various subjects such as fishing, camping, history, fiction, and many others, but this one looked more like one of the journals he'd been reading.

As his fingers rested on the book, a chill crept into them and shot through his arm. It wasn't a feeling that he got from the book itself; it was because he was positive that he heard something bump into the window on the far end of the room.

He moved to the glass to get a better look. It was difficult to see the parking lot in the night from the light reflecting off the inside of the window, so he pressed his forehead to it and cupped his hands around his eyes. The trees swayed in the pale moonlight. Felix's truck sat in front of him. The rest of the parking lot was empty. Mark stood on his toes and craned his neck, but he couldn't see what had made the noise.

Could someone have been watching him? He couldn't be sure; he couldn't even be sure that he heard a noise at all. He was a little jumpy lately, and all things considered, he didn't really blame himself.

Mostly satisfied that it was just his imagination, he returned to the table he was sitting at, but this time he sat on the other side so he could face the window. He opened the black book and began reading it, pausing to glance at the window once in a while.

The book certainly wasn't a journal, but it became clear after the first several pages that it belonged to Nathaniel. Mark's heartbeat quickened. Most of it seemed to be quickly-jotted records of various transactions, but there were also notes of things Nathaniel intended to do. All of it seemed to be in relation to the construction of the lodge and various other facilities he intended to build. Most of the entries were in point form, so Mark had trouble understanding what some of them meant. He thumbed through the book, finding some reminders and a lot of records of debts owed, both incoming and outgoing.

The lights in the room flickered. Mark instinctively looked at the window, but something else was going on. The bulbs in the frosted sconces pulsed and waned, then they went out completely.

The hairs on the back of his neck stood up. The entire lodge was black, except for the moonlight coming through the windows. The air became colder and Mark felt a presence next to him. He let out a miserable moan. Then he heard the intruder's soft breath.

He toppled out of his chair and slammed to the floor. A person stood where he had been, small and glowing.

"Jamie!" Mark gasped. He shivered as he climbed back to his feet, not taking his eyes off the ghost of his son. Before Mark could regain his train of thought, Jamie turned and fled the library. Mark stared a moment in disbelief before chasing after him. He waved his arms out in front of him to feel around in the darkness, but he still managed to ram his leg into one of the tables and rebound off the doorframe before he even got out of the library. Jamie was at the far end of the lounge now, in front of the doors leading to the lake.

"Jamie!" Mark cried, desperate to get his attention. But Jamie ignored him and walked right through the closed doors.

Mark tripped over a stool and nearly crashed to the floor before regaining his footing. He tore open the doors and the cool night air rushed to meet him in the vacuum it created. Jamie was already at the docks. He followed, but no matter how fast he went, Jamie always seemed to be the same distance ahead of him.

"Jamie, stop!" he yelled.

And that he did, at the end of the dock. He stood at the water's edge, staring at the island. Mark screeched to a halt halfway across the dock and beheld him.

"What is it you want me to see?" he asked, exasperated. "What happened on that island?"

Jamie turned and looked at Mark. Then his glowing body faded into the night until all Mark saw were dark waters.

"No!" he yelled. He stomped his foot on the old wood in frustration. There was a fishing boat tied to the dock and he considered taking it to the island right now. He saw the silhouette of it sitting on the water, taunting him. His fist clenched, then he turned away and swung it at the air. "Stupid!" he muttered to himself as he headed back for the lodge to get some sleep. There was something deep inside of him that knew he would have to travel there sooner or later. But not tonight.

As his feet scuffed along the gravel pathway, the nauseating feeling that he was being watched filled him again. He glanced around, seeing dark shapes skulking all around like veiled attackers. When his eyes flitted over to the woods, they stopped on something very tall between the tree trunks. Hunter.

Mark's stomach turned and he nearly vomited. The acid bubbled and turned to rage, his internally burning fire stoked by his frustration. He stopped dead in his tracks and turned his body toward the goliath. He'd been running into nothing but dead ends since coming here, he was frustrated beyond belief that he couldn't communicate with his son, and he was still reeling with all the emotions of losing his family. He had nothing left to lose and now this asshole was taunting him. So Mark headed straight for him.

"*You stupid son of a...*" he muttered viciously, his mouth almost foaming. His feet scuffed off the gravel path and found the grassy incline leading to the woods. "WHAT THE HELL DO YOU WANT FROM ME?!" he bellowed.

Hunter didn't move.

Mark got closer and closer to the dark shape. It wasn't until he got within twenty feet that he realized just how tall Hunter was. He had to be well over seven feet tall. His nerve faltered suddenly, and then after he passed a tree that momentarily obscured his view of the giant, Hunter was gone.

Mark glanced around frantically, but it was no good; he saw only the dark woods. The horrifying realization bubbled up in him that he was alone in the dark with a serial killer.

— CHAPTER ELEVEN —

Up in Smoke

The woods were quiet, the night air still. All around, it seemed like space and time had suspended. Mark stood in the darkness alone. All the hairs on his body stood on end, and for a time he felt in perfect harmony with the environment around him. He listened. He could hear the gentle movement of the lake's water far down at the bottom of the hill. He could hear the boats bumping into the inner walls of the boathouse. He could hear a small woodland creature scamper across the gravel path by the front of the lodge. He could hear a scream.

It came from up the hill, deeper still into the woods. It was a terrible scream, wretched and full of pain. It came from the brothers' house.

Mark took a step toward it, seeing part of the façade through the trees.

The house stood seemingly in opposition of him, challenging him to approach. Its demented figure leaned unnaturally in the pale moonlight. The trees became denser around the house, and they casted twisted shadows across it.

His eyes flicked from window to window, trying to see some sort of light or other evidence of a presence through the tightly-fitted boards.

The faint scream rang out in the night air again.

Felix was right. The brothers were murderers after all. Cleaver and Firebug were in there right now, doing God-knows-what to their poor victim. Mark imagined a hobbled victim futilely crawling across the floor, Cleaver following behind holding a blood-soaked axe. Mark would be joining her soon. He made his final mistake by brashly marching into the woods.

The unmistakable sound of a twig snapping underfoot came from behind him. He spun around, but there was nothing but expansive wilderness.

Another twig, behind him again. He turned, but Hunter was still nowhere to be seen.

A footstep came from his left.

A loud crunch to his right.

He wheeled around in all directions, desperately looking for the source of the sounds. His body began to shake with fear. His legs were weak and he dedicated all the energy he had to keeping himself standing to defend himself.

As the encroaching noises continued, he knew that this was all part of the game for Hunter. Hunter only made his presence known when he wanted to. In every other moment, he was as silent as the night was now, standing in shadows and watching his prey.

Mark's heart hammered. A series of very slow crunches happened one after another, all around him. They seemed to be closing in on him. Frantic, he bent and picked up a sharp branch, brandishing the pointed end around at the smothering woods.

The footsteps closed in, maybe only a few yards away now. Mark continued to spin around, clutching the branch tightly. His heart pounded so hard he thought it would explode. A quick rush of staggered footsteps came up to him from behind and Mark turned and thrust his branch blindly at Hunter.

"JESUS!" his assailant cried as he narrowly deflected Mark's branch then fell to the ground.

Mark came off balance as well and fell next to the man.

Felix groaned and achingly pushed himself to his feet.

"Felix?"

He bent and picked up his cane, then whacked Mark in the leg with it. Mark cried out in pain.

"*What the hell is wrong with you?*" Felix said in a hushed voice. Before Mark could respond, Felix grabbed him by the collar and dragged him toward the lodge. He carefully placed his cane on the ground with every other step as they began to descend the wooded hill.

"*What are you doing up here?*" Felix demanded.

"I saw Hunter standing—"

"*Shh! Not so loud!*"

"*He was standing here, watching me,*" Mark whispered.

"And you decided to what? Go talk to him? Are you out of your mind?"

Mark knew Felix was right; now that his emotions had cooled, he knew it was a dumb thing to do. He was so frustrated at all the dead ends he was encountering and tried to take it out on a serial killer. It made sense at the time.

"*I saw him,*" Mark blurted suddenly.

"*Who?*"

"*My son.*"

"*What?*"

"*I never told you... After I found my family that day, I heard someone in the house with me. It was my son.*"

"*Didn't you say he died, too?*"

"*Yeah, and that's what I can't figure out. When I saw him, he was different... like a ghost. And I've been seeing him in my dreams ever since. It's like he's trying to tell me something. I was in the library, going through Nathaniel's journals, and he suddenly appeared next to me. He wanted me to follow him down to the lake, but when we got there, he just disappeared. I think he wants me to go to that island.*"

Felix didn't say anything. He focused on his footing as the hill became steeper.

Mark kept glancing over his shoulder as they made their way through the woods.

"*There's something else,*" Mark said. "*When I was in the woods here, I heard a scream coming from that house.*"

Felix said nothing and continued down the hill.

"*Did you hear what I said?*" Mark asked.

Felix still said nothing.

"Felix!"

Felix turned around and grabbed him by the collar. "*What do you want me to say, huh? I've heard screams coming from there before, too. There's nothing I can do now. That's all over with.*" He paused, then added, "*And stay the hell away from that island.*"

Felix let go of his shirt and looked around at the woods behind him, then he turned and continued walking.

Mark followed quietly. After several seconds of awkward silence, he said: "*What's with the cane? I haven't seen you use one before.*"

"*My leg doesn't do so well with inclines on its own,*" Felix replied.

They neared the edge of the woods, not far from the lodge now. As they talked to each other, they walked right past Hunter, who was standing three feet to their side. He watched them as they continued down the grassy hill and disappeared into the lodge.

— — —

Mark stared up at the ceiling as the moonlight slowly swept across his room. As he lay on his back, he felt completely comfortable. He couldn't feel his body, but only the warming sensation that flowed through it. He looked toward the foot of his bed.

Jamie was standing there. He was flesh and blood. He beckoned Mark to get up.

Right on command, Mark felt his body rise out of bed.

There was none of the usual happiness or mischief on Jamie's face this time; he carried a somber look about him.

When Mark stood in front of Jamie, watching him with a feeling of curiosity, Jamie turned and slowly walked away. He opened the room's door and disappeared into the hallway.

Mark again tried to call out to him, but his autopilot body remained silent as it casually walked after him.

Out in the hallway now, a strange smell filled his nostrils. It was reminiscent of burning campfires, but he couldn't understand why he smelled that in the lodge. His body pressed on, passing the staircase leading up to the rooms on the second floor.

The lounge was largely dark, but a strange orange light flashed across it.

Mark found himself in the library. Jamie stood in front of him, observing him. Mark's gaze was locked on him, but he fought against this, trying to glimpse other parts of the room. From what he could see in his peripheral vision, there was nothing unusual, despite the orange light. He tried to ask Jamie why he brought him here, but was again reminded of his body's stubbornness.

Jamie showed no emotion on his face. He looked as if he were waiting to make sure Mark was paying attention.

Mark felt like there was something very important he was trying to show him, but he didn't know how.

What is it?! Mark cried in his head.

A shrill beeping noise emitted from somewhere around them.

Jamie erupted into flames. Where a young boy was a moment before, there was now only a pillar of fire in the vague shape of him. He stood still as the flames encased him, his eyes the only recognizable part, peering out from the fire.

Mark felt a sharp panic swell through him. He tried to launch himself toward Jamie, and this time his body was in agreement. He swung out his arms and wrapped Jamie in them. As soon as his flesh touched his burning figure, a horrid pain shot through him.

He jolted out of bed, horrible pain coursing through his body. There was an intense burning in his arms and he held them up to his face, trying to see what was wrong with them.

As his brain eased from the initial panic, he realized he was fine. But the shrill beeping remained, coming from somewhere outside his room. And that burning smell was there, too. He heard the faint sounds of someone yelling.

He bolted toward the door and ripped it open. Orange light danced and flicked all around, coming from the library. He rounded the corner and was met with the sight of the library in flames as a wave of intense heat rushed over him. The bookshelves on both sides and the two long tables in the middle of the room were on fire. Felix held a fire extinguisher, battling the flames engulfing the bookshelf on the right side of the room. He glanced over his shoulder and saw Mark.

"There's another extinguisher in the kitchen!" he yelled. "And a fire blanket, too! In the cabinet under the sink!"

Mark took off through the lounge. His hand slapped on the kitchen wall until he found the light switch and the bright fluorescents hummed. The fire extinguisher hung on a hook next to him. Its red hue was unmistakable in the otherwise stark white kitchen. Cradling it under his arm, he pulled open the cabinet doors beneath the sink. A neatly-folded but very dusty brown and speckled blanket was wedged in the far corner. Mark grabbed it and ran to the library.

Felix was still fighting the fire on the right side. Mark didn't have time to notice how he was doing and instead dumped the extinguisher on the floor and got to work. He unfolded the blanket and held it out wide with both hands, then tossed it across the first table, trying to stay away from the unbearable flames. The blanket fluttered momentarily over it then covered its surface, snuffing out the fire. He circled around it and patted the edges of the blanket to make sure the blaze was out, then he pulled it off and threw it over the second table. The fire engulfing the bookshelves was spreading and Felix yelled for help.

Noxious smoke rolled through the room like a slow wave and Felix started hacking, stumbling from his fireman duties and trying to get some air. Mark picked up a chair and hurled it at the plate glass window at the back of the room. The glass shattered and the smoke rolled out, climbing up into the night.

With the smog thinning, Mark picked up his extinguisher and patted Felix on the shoulder. Felix gave him a nod and the two of them went to work on one of the bookshelves. The fire had covered nearly all of the books, but if they let it spread any more, it would take the whole lodge.

The flame seemed to wax and wane as they battled it. All the while, their skin blistered as they glanced over their shoulders at the encroaching inferno on the other bookshelf. They got the first fire down enough that Mark could break free and tackle the other one.

He struggled, trying to spray the chemicals around the edges of the fire to contain it. Despite his best efforts, it slowly spread. "Felix!" he yelled, sweat pouring down his face. He crouched low, trying to stay under the smoke that stung his eyes so he could see. The blaze was too much, and he was about to fall to his knees in fatigue, when a hand slapped him on the shoulder. He glanced and saw Felix's wiry smile next to him. The fire on the other shelf extinguished completely, Felix aimed his nozzle and tag-teamed the last flames with Mark.

When it was out, they both stumbled to the lounge and collapsed on a black leather couch next to the pool table. The smoke eventually cleared out and the fire alarm fell silent.

"What the hell happened?" Mark asked at last.

Felix craned his head toward him with his mouth hanging open, still out of breath. "The fire alarm... woke me up. I came out and the library was... in flames." Before Mark had a chance to think of the implications of it, Felix added: "It was Firebug."

Mark looked at him with sharp eyes. "Are you sure?"

"There's no doubt about it," Felix said.

"Why would he try to burn this place down?"

"I don't know," Felix said. "But I'd wager my last dollar it has something to do with you." Felix chuckled but couldn't quite hide the sound of bitterness. He patted his breast pocket, but he was out of toothpicks, so he laid his head back on the couch and closed his eyes. "I don't think Firebug wanted to burn the whole lodge," he added.

"What do you mean?"

"If he really wanted to burn it all down, he would have doused everything in kerosene first. He always does that. If he did that here, there's no way we could have put it out."

Mark thought about it and realized Felix was right.

"But why did he pick the library, specifically?" Felix asked himself.

Mark was struck with a sudden realization. "When I was reading Nathaniel's journals, I swear someone was watching me from the window."

"Did you see him?"

"No. When I looked at the window, there was no one there. I thought I was imagining things, but maybe he really was out there. He must have seen what I was reading."

"One of the journals?" Felix asked.

"No. I found a secret ledger that belonged to Nathaniel hidden in the corner of a shelf. That's when I felt like someone was watching me. I heard a noise on the window, like something bumped into it. Firebug must have seen me finding something I wasn't supposed to see."

"Then they *are* working for Nathaniel," Felix said.

"They must not want his secrets to get out," Mark reasoned. "There must be something important in that ledger."

Felix shrugged. "What does it matter now? It was burned up in the fire."

"No it wasn't," Mark said with a sheepish grin on his face.

"It wasn't?"

"After you brought me back to the lodge, I grabbed it from the table in the library and brought it with me to my room. I left the journals there, but the ledger came with me. There's got to be something big in there."

Felix's face became strained, thinking of the implications. Then the strain washed away and he stood up. "I should call the fire department."

— CHAPTER TWELVE —

Digging up the Past

The sun had just crept over the horizon when the fire department arrived. As firefighters traipsed back and forth through the lodge, examining the damage in the library, Mark hid himself away in his room, drinking.

He was exhausted from lack of sleep and recent events became overwhelming for him. After he and Felix put out the fire, he wandered around the lodge aimlessly, unable to rest. He skimmed through Nathaniel's secret black ledger, but he couldn't find anything of use. Hector stopped by early in the morning to see what the commotion was about, then left to pick up some things at the market in town. When the fire department showed up, Mark went to the bar and surreptitiously grabbed a few beers then retreated to his room.

He sat on the edge of the bed, pouring them down. The taste was still awful to him, but they brought him comfort; there was a certain nihilism in drinking to him that he didn't like, but—now that he lost everything— had embraced. It also helped numb the burning questions swirling around his head. He couldn't understand why the brothers would want to bring him here only to terrorize and harass him for getting too close to the truth.

He thought about Firebug. If only he'd looked at the window just a split second sooner, maybe he would have seen him. But it didn't really matter; Felix firmly told him not to make any mention of Firebug to the fire department or the police. He wasn't sure if this was because Felix was truly finished involving himself in the brothers' affairs, or if he just wanted everyone else to think so.

The beer bottle in Mark's hand contained a thin layer of liquid, and he looked at it morosely before downing the contents. He tossed the empty bottle behind him onto the bed. He wasn't very proud of the fact that he'd now taken up drinking, but he just couldn't bring himself to care about much of anything when he felt this defeated. What was even more alarming to him was that he was strangely starting to enjoy it. He wondered where that elusive thin line was that his father had crossed when it came to alcohol.

He reached over to the writing desk and grabbed the picture frame with his family in it. He looked at the scratchy red 'X's drawn over each face. Rage flooded within him and he swung the frame down onto the corner of the desk. The unmistakable sound of fracturing glass rang out in the otherwise silent room. He slowly turned the frame over with a shaky hand. The image of his family was unrecognizable now, covered with a spider web of cracks. He felt a deep wave of depression sweep over him and he weakly tossed the picture frame onto the floor. He eyed the last remaining bottle of beer that he stole from the bar, but only shook his head after consideration.

He felt utterly useless. It was his basic duty as a husband and a father to protect his wife and children. But he couldn't even do that right. It was the most horrible mistake he could make, and he let it happen. Now he was here in this lodge, chasing his own tail, trying to figure out how and why the place had a connection to what happened to his family. And he just couldn't shake the images of Jamie, both in his dreams and in real life, as hard as it was to believe what he saw was even possible. His son was trying to tell him something, but he couldn't even understand something simple like that. He felt as though he were the very definition of failure.

The fact that he had vague memories of the lodge was equally as troubling. He was positive he'd never even been to South Carolina before, yet every once in a while he'd get subtle feelings of déjà vu. They mostly seemed to happen whenever he encountered Jamie. Maybe they were Jamie's memories, somehow being transferred to him. Maybe it was the only way Jamie could communicate to him. But when did Jamie ever come here? As his father, he obviously would have known if Jamie was brought to this place.

He rubbed his temples. An idea, innocent enough, crept up into his mind. He paused, considering it. He was chasing a long shot, but he didn't have much else.

He pushed himself to his feet and made his way out to the lounge. Felix was standing in the library, looking over the damage. "Felix, could I talk to you for a minute?" he asked.

Felix turned around, startled out of his thoughts. "Hmm, what?" His brain took a moment to process what Mark said, then he added: "Yeah, sure." He followed Mark into the empty dining room.

"I was wondering..." Mark said. "You said you've owned this lodge for about thirty years, right?"

Felix nodded. "Thirty years this summer."

"This might sound a little weird, but... do you remember me ever staying here before?"

"I... can't say that I do," Felix said slowly. He looked confused.

"Maybe I might have looked a little different back then, and I would've been with my son, a small little boy?" Mark felt himself really grasping at straws. As he said each word, he felt stupider and stupider, but he pressed on. "I might have had a daughter, too... and a wife?"

Felix became visibly apprehensive. "I really don't, Mark. And I don't know what you're getting at. What's this all about?"

"I don't know. Maybe it's nothing. I just keep getting this feeling that I've been here before, but I just can't remember. Do you have any old guest registries?"

"Yeah, I suppose so. I should have registries going back to when I bought this place. Must be in a box somewhere."

"Would you mind if I had a look at them?"

"No, knock yourself out," Felix said. "Let me take a look for 'em." He disappeared down the hall toward the guest rooms.

While Mark waited, he walked over to the window and looked out at the landscape. The lake was very tranquil. There was no sign of Pete, but he figured that it was probably a little earlier than he normally fished. He stepped out into the lounge and looked at the clock hanging on the wall above the bar.

Nearly eight o'clock.

The sound of Felix's boots crescendoed from the hallway and he reappeared a few seconds later holding a large, dusty box. He walked up to the bar and dropped it on top.

"Well, there you go," Felix said. "That's all of 'em, going back thirty years ago. If you want any older than that, you're shit out of luck."

Mark stepped toward the box and peered over the edge of it. It was filled with long, hard-bound ledgers of varying sizes and colors. There must have been at least twenty-five of them. He started to regret his request when he realized what a monumental amount of work it would be to read through them all.

"Just remember that you brought this on yourself," Felix said with a smile before turning and walking away to what was left of the library.

"Thanks," Mark muttered as he stared at the registries, mesmerized. He suddenly felt like he needed alcohol again. He pushed away this feeling and took a seat, then dumped the box across the bar top and began organizing the registries chronologically.

He reached for one and looked at the date of the first entry.

Jensen – September 4, 2016 – 3 nights

He ran a finger down the rest of the page, going over each name, carefully but quickly. He flipped through the pages as fast as he could, but it still took him twenty minutes to get through the whole registry. He spent the next two hours painstakingly poring over them. At the end of it, he'd only managed to get through seven of them. He counted twenty-one registries left. He slumped his head on the bar. "Damn it," he muttered.

It was useless. It was a needle in a haystack. If he was convinced that he'd never been here before, then he could look through all of them and wind up with nothing but a waste of time on his hands.

He slid the oldest registry over to him and opened it.

Kowalski – Tuesday, June 9, 1987 – second suite, 4 nights

This must be the very first person to stay here after Felix bought the place, Mark thought. He took quick glances around at some of the entries before flipping to another page. That's when he saw it:

Winters – Wednesday, June 24, 1987 – first suite, 5 nights

Now that he'd finally found the name he was looking for, a sudden disappointment set in. All it was was a last name. It could have been anyone. Plus it was from thirty years ago, which would put him at six years old. It couldn't possibly have been him. Still, he was striking out left and right; what was one more?

He got up and returned to the library where Felix was just finishing up talking to the fire chief.

"Felix," Mark said, tapping his shoulder.

Felix turned. "What's up?"

"1987. That's the first year you owned the place, right?"

"Right."

"Do you remember anything unusual happening that summer?"

Felix didn't even have to think about it. "Of course."

Mark was taken aback by his quickness in answering. "What happened?"

"I will never, for as long as I live, forget that first summer. It was the summer when a man killed his son. Didn't I tell you about that?"

"You mentioned it," Mark said, transfixed on every word he said. "Why did he do that?"

"I remember I was cleaning up dishes in the kitchen. That's when I heard the screams. I dropped a plate, they made me jump so bad. I ran up to the window and looked outside. It was coming from somewhere out on the grounds, but I didn't know where. Just about the same time, the boy's father ran outside. I followed along, as quick as my leg would allow me," he said, patting his leg.

"The scream was coming from that island off on the lake. It was the man's little boy. He kept screaming over and over again. The man took a fishing boat out to the lake and went over there. I just stood by the docks, waiting. I don't think I've ever felt so nervous in my whole life.

"After a while, the screaming stopped. Then someone else started screaming. But this one was different; it was full of emotion. I don't know that I've ever heard such a wretched sound before. Eventually, the boat came back and the man had his kid in his arms, dead. He was howling bloody murder."

"What happened to the kid?" Mark asked.

"His dad found him on the island. The island changed him; made him feral. The kid attacked his father on sight. He apparently had superhuman strength, as the man described it. Said he had no choice but to break his boy's neck. It wasn't until he laid his son on the ground that I saw the damage that was done. His boy tore something fierce out of his chest. His shirt was soaked in blood. But he stayed conscious. I don't know how."

Mark considered what he was about to say very carefully, knowing it was crazy. "How old was the son?"

"About five or six, maybe."

"Do you remember his name?"

Felix thought about this for a few seconds, then said: "Jamie."

Mark was stunned. A red-hot feeling surged through his body and he became lightheaded. He put a hand on the wall to keep himself from falling over. "What was his father's name?"

Felix once again thought about it, this time taking a little bit longer to come up with an answer. When he was about to reply, a foreign voice came from over Mark's shoulder.

"Well shoot, sure is a mess in here."

Felix and Mark turned.

"You got that right, Hank," Felix said.

Hank was a plump man who looked to be in his late fifties, wearing a Clemington Sheriff's uniform. He walked past Mark and looked at him with a suspicious, almost repugnant look.

"How the hell did this happen, Felix?" Hank asked, craning his head in every direction, taking a look at the damage.

"Someone must've broke in last night and tried to torch the place," Felix said.

"Do you have any idea who that might be?" Hank asked.

"Not a clue," Felix said, shooting a look at Mark.

Hank continued to ask Felix about the fire as he walked over to the broken window and looked outside.

Felix glanced at Mark, knowing that he was dying for more information about what happened thirty years ago. "Go talk to Hector, Mark. He was there that day, too. He probably knows more about it than I do, in fact."

Mark nodded his appreciation and went on his way.

Was it really possible? Did his son really die thirty years ago? Was he the father who snapped his son's neck? It was ridiculous, but there was that dream about the cabin on the island and the terrible screams from within. That's what Jamie had been trying to show him. Somehow, maybe that was what happened thirty years ago.

— CHAPTER THIRTEEN —

Revelations

Mark pounded his fist on Hector's front door. He waited impatiently for him to answer. He pounded again. "Hector!"

He pressed his ear to the door and listened. There was nothing but silence on the other side. He walked around the cottage to the back and pressed his face to one of the sunroom's windows, using his hands to shield his eyes from the morning sun above.

The sunroom sat empty, as did the parts of the living room and kitchen that he could make out from this angle.

Just then, the sound of stones being chewed up came from off in the distance. His head perked up, and he went around to the front of the cottage again. The sound came closer, and the low hum of an engine winded up an out-of-sight road until it came to a stop behind a row of dense trees ahead. The engine cut out and a door opened. Mark walked along a narrow dirt trail and around the trees.

Hector clamped his straw hat down onto his head with one hand as he ducked out of the Jeep's interior.

Under his other arm, he wrestled a large brown bag of groceries out with him.

"Hector," Mark said.

Hector, having still not noticed him, let out a startled cry and fell backward against the driver's seat. His grocery bag tipped with him and a few tomatoes spilled out into the Jeep. Hector lay back against the seat, looking up at the sky in a daze. His eyes darted back and forth, like he was still trying to figure out what had happened.

Mark rushed over to him and helped him up. "Hector, it's me."

Hector tilted his head toward Mark and after a couple seconds, his look of bewilderment changed to warm recognition. "Oh, Mark... you scared me."

Mark feigned a smile, distracted by all the questions racing through his mind. "There's something important I need to talk to you about," he said. He looked past Hector and saw the tomatoes lying on the floor of the Jeep. "Jeez, I'm sorry, Hector." He bent into the interior and grabbed them all, carefully placing them into Hector's grocery bag.

Hector patted him on the shoulder in appreciation. "Come on," he said, "let's go inside."

A cool breeze greeted them as they stepped into the cottage. It was very refreshing as sweat started to drip from Mark's forehead from the sweltering sun.

"Please, have a seat," Hector said.

Mark shook his head and started to pace. "I need to know about what happened thirty years ago." After going a few lengths of the living room, he stopped behind the oversized armchair and leaned against it. "That summer when a guest at the lodge killed his son. Felix told me you were there."

Hector seemed to ignore him and said, "Can I get you something to drink? Lemonade, maybe? I made some fresh this morning!"

Mark considered, but he said, "No... no, I'm okay, thanks."

Hector once again frowned at his declination to a drink. He shuffled around and sat down on the opposing armchair. He took off his hat and slicked his sweaty hair back, then pressed the hat back down. "All right, then. What did you want to talk about?"

Mark followed Hector's lead without thinking and sat down on the armchair. "The man killing his son here."

Hector looked confused. "Why would you want to know about that?"

"Because I keep having dreams of this place, but I can't remember ever coming here. I keep seeing my son in these dreams, and every time, he's trying to tell me about that island on the lake. He's trying to tell me that something bad happened to him in that cabin. It doesn't make any sense, but I keep seeing him as a ghost when I'm not dreaming. He tried bringing me to the docks then he just kept looking at the island. He wants me to go there."

As Mark talked, Hector became increasingly suspicious, like he was slowly formulating a thought.

"I looked through some of the guest registries that Felix had for the lodge going back thirty years, and I found my name in one of them. It was from thirty years ago, and Felix told me about what happened that summer. A boy wandered into that cabin and came out different. He attacked his father and his father killed him. Felix said the boy's name was Jamie."

A warm look came over Hector's face. "My God, boy," he said. "Is it really you?" He placed a hand on his cheek and became lost in reverie.

"What?" Mark said quietly.

"You were there and you don't remember it," Hector said, shaking his head in pity. "That man from thirty years ago was your father, Bruce. And the Jamie that's haunting your dreams isn't your son; he was your brother."

The room seemed to warp in front of Mark. "I... had a brother?"

"No one would blame you," Hector replied. "To witness something as traumatic as you did and not block it out would be a miracle. After all, you were only a little boy at the time."

Mark sat in stunned silence, not knowing what to say.

"Jamie was your little brother," Hector continued. "I think he was about five when he came here. Your father brought you and your brother here on vacation all those years ago." He studied Mark. "Can you recall anything now?"

Mark sat for a long moment. "Jesus," he said. He felt a sudden shortness of breath and his entire body began trembling. As if the floodgates of his mind had opened, memories began pouring into his consciousness, overpowering every other thought he tried to have. The shaking became violent and he had to crouch forward in his chair and hold his head in his hands to keep himself together.

Hector bent forward and put a firm hand on Mark's shoulder. "Do you remember?" he insisted.

"I do. Jesus, I do. I remember everything."

— — —

Mark peeked around the tree. Jamie slowly wandered through the woods, alert and on edge. Mark moved from trunk to trunk, being careful where he stepped, so as not to betray his presence.

"Where are you?" Jamie called out. He spun around in circles, searching in all directions for his big brother.

A smile spread over Mark's face and he rushed out from behind a tree. He dove into Jamie from behind and they tumbled to the ground, rolling across the dirty terrain.

"RAAAWR!" Mark yelled as he wrestled with Jamie. Jamie giggled. They started to roll down the decline of the hill, bumping up against trees and underbrush on the way. Eventually they came to a stop and got up. They brushed the dirt off their clothes and set off down the rest of the hill toward the lodge.

It was one of the hottest summers in recent memory, and their father, Bruce, had taken them down to Hollow's Cove for a fun weekend. Mark and Jamie were so happy when they first arrived after the long car ride from Tennessee. They settled right in and began playing on the lodge's grounds while their father checked in and brought their luggage to their room. The lodge was bustling with activity. Several boats sat on the water with families fishing and enjoying the weather. Felix worked with a diligent staff of assistants, covering a wide range of responsibilities to keep everything running smoothly.

"Where's Hulk?" Mark asked.

A look of near terror suddenly washed over Jamie's face. He ran over to the lodge and then back up the hill, frantically searching in bushes and behind rocks. Mark stood and watched from a distance as a devilish smile crept over his face. He reached into the side pocket of his cargo shorts and pulled out an Incredible Hulk action figure.

"Hulk... SMASH!" he yelled as he held up the action figure and played with its adjustable arms.

Jamie spun around and his panicked look faded. "Give it back!" he yelled as he ran toward Mark.

Mark took off down the gravel path for the docks. "You're gonna have to catch me!"

He ran the length of the closest one stretching over the water. There was an old rowboat tied to the end of the dock and Mark stopped just in front of it, turning to face Jamie.

Five motorboats sat out on the lake, filled with families trying to catch the afternoon's bass. The previous owner of the lodge kept the sole rowboat tied to the dock as an old-fashioned backup, and Felix kept that tradition.

Mark jumped into the boat. "*Hulk wants a boat ride!*" he growled in his best Hulk impression. He bent forward and stood Hulk on the wooden seat in front of him.

Jamie giggled and hopped into the boat, too. He grabbed the toy from Mark and started playing with it, pretending that it was lifting one end of an oar at one point, and then he dipped his arm over the side of the boat to simulate it swimming at another.

Mark untied the knot tethering the boat to the dock. The boat began to drift out on the water. He grabbed one of the oars. "Come on!" he said. He looked over his shoulder at the island sitting on the far end of the cove. "Let's go there!"

"But we're not supposed to!" Jamie said.

"But I wanna!" Mark retorted. "It'll be fun!" When he saw that Jamie still wasn't convinced, he said: "Hulk wants to go there, too!"

Jamie smiled at this and grabbed the other oar. The two of them slowly churned through the water, and the boat crept toward the island. The families in the other boats didn't seem to notice them as they rowed by. The cove was large and it took them a long time to cross it and reach the island. When they did, their arms were exhausted and they sat in the boat for a few minutes before getting out. They waded through shallow water until they were standing on the shore. A hill extended up in front of them. It cut off their view from the rest of the island beyond it, but immediately they noticed a thick murk that hung over the area. The trees were unnaturally blackened and twisted into strange formations. The dirt underfoot had an odd, grayish color to it, almost as if a sheet of ash had fallen onto the ground.

"Come on, let's go!" Mark said to Jamie as he climbed up the hill. Jamie followed, the Hulk action figure gripped tightly in his hand.

As they went, they began to notice each peculiarity of the island, but kept their thoughts to themselves. Aside from the lifeless surroundings, the sun overhead seemed unable to penetrate through the trees, as if some invisible barrier distorted it and only allowed a diffused, murky light through. They crested the hill and looked at the island in front of them. The hill immediately began to slope back down on the other side. A trail ran down the middle of it between the looming trees. Just after it petered off into flat ground, the trail narrowed and made a sharp turn to the left, disappearing behind more unnatural-looking trees. As quickly as they had clambered up the hill, they were just as quickly stopped dead in their tracks.

"What's down there?" Jamie asked.

"I don't know," Mark replied absentmindedly. He was terrified of it. All of his good humor drained from him and he wanted desperately to go back across the cove. But at the same time, he was incredibly curious about what was down there. When they first came to the lodge, Felix warned them that the island was off-limits. He wanted to know why.

"Go see what's down there," Mark said.

Jamie turned suddenly as if someone just slapped him. "No!" he cried. A deep sense of pleading prevailed in his eyes.

"Just see what's there and come right back."

"*No*," Jamie croaked. He began to sob, streams of tears rolling down his face and staining his red shirt. "I don't wanna be here anymore. I wanna go back."

"Do it!" Mark said, giving Jamie a shove.

Jamie became frantic as he fought to regain his balance. He steadied his footing and his sobs became uncontrollable.

Mark had a terrible feeling in the pit of his stomach for how he was treating his brother. He wanted so badly to see what was around the corner at the bottom of the hill, but he was terrified to go himself. He looked at Jamie with pity, then steeled himself against what he was about to do. He quickly snatched Jamie's Incredible Hulk toy from his hand. Jamie only had time to look at him in shock before he threw the toy down the hill.

Hulk sailed through the air and bounced down the trail. It rolled and rolled until it finally came to rest on the flat ground, right where the trail curved to the left and disappeared.

Jamie sank to his knees, throwing his body on the ground and wailing. He made a horrible, guttural noise. But eventually he lifted his head and looked at the toy, far away in the clutches of this evil island. Then he rose to his feet and started down.

Mark pleaded in his head for Jamie not to go; that he was sorry. But he made no sound. He cried as he watched his brother slowly make his way down the trail.

When Jamie reached the toy, he bent and picked it up. He started to turn back for the hill, but he stopped partway.

Mark's stomach twisted into a knot when he realized Jamie was staring at the trail behind the trees. Jamie just stood there motionlessly as if he were transfixed.

"What do you see?" Mark yelled down nervously.

Jamie ignored him.

"What's there?" Mark yelled.

And then Jamie dropped his Hulk toy and disappeared around the bend.

"*Jamie?*" Mark said quietly, his nose running. He waited, but his brother didn't come back. Panic swelling in him, he took off down the hill, his fear of what would happen to his brother more intense than his fear of what would happen to him. When he got to the bend in the trail, he stopped.

Jamie was off in the distance, slowly walking along the path. The trees lining either side became more misshapen as the path went on. Eventually, they turned into a bizarre mockery of nature's intention.

The trail ended at a dilapidated cabin far in the distance. Jamie started to walk up its sagging and splintered steps leading to a porch. The windowless structure bore down on him like an unspeakable evil.

Mark shivered. He could feel that the very core of the chill was at the heart of the cabin. "Jamie, *don't*," he croaked.

He was on the porch now, nearing the door.

"*Don't*," Mark whispered. He was too frozen by his fear to do anything but watch as Jamie opened the door. It opened onto complete blackness as a blast of icy air poured out and swept along the trail. Then Jamie stepped into the blackness and disappeared. The door of the cabin slammed shut.

Mark's heart jumped into his throat as he waited in silence. He took a step forward. "Jamie?"

A shrill scream erupted inside the cabin.

Mark's body locked up.

Another scream rang through the empty air, more terrible and full of pain than the first. Mark had never heard anything like it come from his brother before. It sounded like he was being tortured.

The screams took on a hysterical quality, like Jamie had been pushed past the point of insanity. They transformed in their resonance until Jamie didn't even sound human anymore.

Mark turned and ran as fast as he could. His feet slipped in the dirt as he frantically clawed his way up the hill back to the shore.

The boat that they'd come to the island in was floating twenty feet out on the water. They never knew to pull it up on shore to prevent it from slipping back into the lake, and now it was slowly drifting toward the lodge without him.

He ran after it, thrashing wildly through the water. He hadn't even learned how to swim yet, and he struggled to reach the boat. As the disturbed water bobbed over his eyes, he caught a glimpse of a boat approaching the island. Just as he began to go under, an arm hoisted him out of the water and pulled him into a boat.

"What are you doing?!" his father yelled. Mark looked up and recognized him. "Where's your brother?!"

Mark tried to unleash a tirade of words that would explain, but he couldn't manage anything, so he just pointed.

Bruce jumped out of the boat and sprinted up the hill. The screaming inside the cabin had stopped by now, but Bruce had heard it clear as day from across the lake.

Mark followed him on shaky legs, feeling safe in the company of his father; he would take care of the situation and make sure his brother was okay. But when he reached the bottom of the hill and saw his father stopped dead in his tracks around the bend, shaking in fear, the small light inside Mark was snuffed out.

The cabin door had opened and Jamie came out. His head was bowed and lilting about as he descended the steps from the porch.

"Jamie!" Bruce yelled. There was fear and confusion in his voice. He wanted to run to his son, but there was something odd about his appearance that kept him rooted to the spot.

Mark shivered miserably as the island's frigid air wrapped around his wet body.

Jamie started down the trail, something peculiar about the way he walked.

Bruce slowly walked forward, holding out his hand. "Jamie?" he said softly.

Jamie stopped. He tilted his head up at last and looked at his father. His mouth hung open and he panted like a dog. His eyes were glazed over and he appeared disoriented. Then his mouth twisted into a snarl, not like a human, but like a feral animal.

Bruce only had enough time to realize his son had lost his mind before Jamie lunged at him. He was so shocked that he couldn't even brace for the impact. Jamie jumped and clung onto his upper body. Bruce staggered backward and tumbled to the ground. Jamie started in on him, fiercely slashing his clawed fingers at his chest. Bruce feebly tried to push him away, but Jamie's strength was enormous. Blood oozed from deep wounds beneath his torn shirt as Bruce fought off the shock. He managed to bridge his hips and throw Jamie off, inadvertently causing him to roll along the ground toward Mark. Jamie recovered faster than he expected and swung his head around wildly, looking for his closest victim.

Mark sat on the forest floor, curled up into a ball and peeking through his fingers. His jaw dropped as Jamie set off for him.

"No!" Bruce cried.

Jamie launched forward like a missile, but Bruce caught the cuff of his pants and made him slam into the ground. His bloody nails dug through the dirt, clawing his way closer and closer to Mark as Bruce struggled to hold him back. Jamie's face was unrecognizable; his eyes were bloodshot, his teeth foaming and gnashing. Mark's little brother was gone.

Bruce held onto his son's pant leg with both hands, digging his heels into the ground and trying to keep him from getting to Mark. "Mark, *run!*" he cried desperately. But Mark was immobilized by the sheer terror he felt.

Jamie inched closer as Mark curled up more. His hunger was insatiable, and soon he would devour him.

"*Stop!*" Bruce screamed. He sobbed, exhausted and afraid that he wouldn't be able to stop him.

Jamie was a few feet away from Mark now. Bruce threw himself down on Jamie's back, but still he crawled forward. The last image Mark saw was Jamie's terrible face contorted into something completely inhuman, inches away from his own.

And then Bruce snapped Jamie's neck.

The terrible force animating him ceased immediately. His body slumped and splayed out.

The last memory Mark had, getting fuzzy now, was of his father hunched over his brother's dead body, screaming.

Then he passed out.

— CHAPTER FOURTEEN —

Putting the Pieces Together

"That's all I remember," Mark said.

Hector leaned forward and patted him on the leg. "It's a terrible thing that happened to you," he said. "I was there when your father came back across the cove. At first I thought you *and* your brother were dead, but you simply fainted from the shock. No one would blame you, of course. I'm amazed that you stayed conscious for that long. Frankly, if—"

"They should," Mark said abruptly.

Hector looked confused. "I'm sorry?"

"They should blame me," Mark said. "For everything." Hector started to speak, but Mark cut him off again. "I killed my brother," he said, realizing the increasing weight of his words. "I brought us to that island. I made him go down there. He *trusted* me. But I made him. And now he's dead. He's been dead so long I didn't even remember I had a brother."

"For God's sake, Mark!" Hector said. "You were six years old! You did nothing more than any other six-year-old would have done. You can't blame yourself for that. I'm sure your father raised you better than that."

Mark's eyes turned cold. "My *father* didn't raise me at all. Between the alcohol and the beatings, he didn't have time to teach me much of anything."

"What?" Hector said, confused. "What do you mean? Surely he never did those things."

Mark let out a sarcastic laugh. "And you would know how?"

Hector looked like he'd just been accused of something terrible. "When you stayed here all those years ago, I befriended your father and spoke with him at length about history. He was a bit of a nut about it, just like me. Mark," he said, planting a firm hand on his leg, "he was perhaps the nicest man I've ever met."

"*What?*" Mark said, appalled.

"I saw the way he played with you and your brother. He was more like your friend than your father."

"Bull."

"Mark, you just described to me how upset he was when your brother died."

"And he probably blamed me for it all those years. Hell, he was right to. Maybe I got what I deserved," Mark said bitterly.

"No," Hector said, holding up his hand, becoming genuinely angry. "Whatever became of your father after that event, he wasn't the same person. You read the journals that I gave you, didn't you?"

Mark nodded.

"Then you must know what that island does to people," Hector said. "It changes them. They become violent... in the case of your brother, rabid. Your father wasn't on that island for very long, but he must have been there just enough to suffer some effects from it. With mild afflictions it could cause a man to be prone to occasional violence and to abuse alcohol. I just want you to know that your father was a good man."

Mark couldn't believe it. Was it possible that his whole life his father's mind had been warped by the consuming presence on that island? If it was, then that made two deaths he was responsible for, both members of his own family.

His family.

The bodies of his wife and children flashed before his eyes and he now realized he was responsible for the deaths of everyone he ever loved. Grief overtook him and he slumped forward, sobbing into his hands.

"I'm so sorry, Mark," Hector said. He braced himself, not sure if he was about to strike a nerve. "You should talk to your father again. Tell him you understand and accept him. I know it's a difficult thought, but if he's still there under the turbulent surface, I'm sure he'd appreciate it."

Mark straightened up. "He's dead."

Hector was shocked. "How?"

"He killed himself."

Hector looked severely distraught. "I'm... I'm sorry," he said softly, looking anywhere in the room other than at Mark.

After several moments of silence, Mark asked: "Why were the three of us so different on the island, then? Why did my father become abusive and nothing happened to me?"

"Everybody reacts differently to the influence on the island," Hector said. "It seems some have a stronger mind than others, more able to resist the persuasion. It sounds like your brother's affliction was compounded by the intensity of the presence inside that cabin. And you... well, maybe your mind is very resistant to the effects that it has. I would count you lucky."

"What's *in* that cabin?" Mark asked.

"I don't know," Hector replied. "I don't think anyone knows."

"Did the police never investigate?"

Hector shook his head. "That island is legend. It's completely shrouded in mystery and that's all it will ever be to the locals. They know not to go anywhere near it. My father taught me that when I was very young."

"So you've never been there?" Mark asked, thinking of the cloaked figure that he saw on the shore of the island two nights before.

"No," Hector replied. He suddenly looked embarrassed. "I'm afraid of water."

"And you live on a lake?"

Hector laughed. "I have no problem being around water—it's a lovely view, of course—I just don't want to get too close to it."

"Why are you afraid of water?"

Hector looked uncertain for a moment. "All right, I suppose I can tell you. A great many years ago, long before Felix ever came to own the lodge, I was taking a stroll along the lake early one morning. I happened to spot a very beautiful young woman skinny-dipping in the lake. I watched her for a minute or two, and then something went wrong. She had swum too far out and she started thrashing, trying to keep herself afloat. After I realized she was drowning, I dove into the water and swam out to her. But by the time I got there, she was already gone. It was the most terrifying experience of my life, and I could never bring myself to go in the lake again."

"Who was she?" Mark asked.

"No one knew. She was by herself, and the police couldn't identify her. She was a Jane Doe as far as they were concerned."

Mark tried to think of something to say, but after remembering what happened to him and his family on the island, something like "I'm sorry to hear that" seemed insincere.

But it was Hector who broke the silence. "If there's ever anything else you need, don't hesitate to come see me."

"There is," Mark said. "Now that I found out the ghost who's been haunting me is my brother and not my son, that still doesn't change anything. He wants me to go to that island. He wants me to help him."

"Mark, please don't go there," Hector said, worry growing in his voice. "The island didn't affect you before, but that's not a guarantee that it won't now. Just, please, until we find out more about what exactly is there, stay away from it."

"The journals that you gave me stopped short of describing why Nathaniel wanted a cabin in the woods, other than to 'study' the island's presence in it. Does he say what he used it for in his other journals?"

"No. For whatever reason, he kept pretty tight-lipped about it. His other journals describe some of his ideas, but he doesn't get too specific about anything."

Mark frowned. "So what am I supposed to do about my brother? Is this all just my mind playing tricks on me, or is he still here somehow?"

"He's still here," Hector said. "Nathaniel made mention that the souls of the people who succumbed to the island's evil and died here are trapped here, made to wander aimlessly in an unending, torturous existence. But he found a way to contain and control the restless spirits. I don't know how, but he's hinted at it."

"Is there anything I can do to help Jamie?"

"I don't know," Hector admitted. "I'll keep digging around. But... there's one other thing."

"What?"

"I think I know how your family died."

"How?" Mark asked, taken aback.

"When I was still working under the assumption that the apparition you were seeing was your son, I was a little unsure of my theory, but now that I know it's your brother, I'm certain of it."

"What theory?"

"When I was reading one of Nathaniel's journals last night, I came across a specific passage where he mentioned using an object to direct a spirit to a certain place. He said that if you take an object that was of great importance to the spirit when they were alive and place a dark incantation on it, that spirit will be bound to the object and will be able to go wherever the object goes."

Mark was confused. He didn't understand what that had to do with the murder of his family.

"When you left for work that morning," Hector continued, "you mentioned that there was a brochure on your porch. Was there anything else there that you might have taken in the house?"

Mark felt like he was just struck by a ton of bricks. "The Incredible Hulk toy. Jamie's Hulk toy," he said breathlessly. "I thought it was my son's and I just tossed it in the rec room."

Hector nodded like Mark just confirmed the suspicion he'd had all along. "Nathaniel noted that these spirits have the ability to materialize at will and they can even affect physical matter. He said that the only function these insane and broken spirits have left is to kill."

Mark's jaw dropped. "You're saying... Jamie killed them? It wasn't one of the brothers up the hill?"

"I'm afraid so," Hector replied. "Just... please know that it's not his fault."

"It's my fault," Mark said.

"No," Hector rebutted, "it's Nathaniel's fault, or whoever it is that's working to resurrect him. They're the ones that killed your family. I can't understand why, but it wasn't your brother's fault; he was being used like a pawn."

"Why hasn't Jamie killed me, then?"

"My best guess is that he won't harm you because he knows you. And he knows that you're the only one who might be able to help him. Deep down, the real Jamie must be there somewhere, reaching out for you."

The two of them sat awhile longer, finishing their conversation as the sun rose up into the budding afternoon sky. Mark left and went back to the lodge. On his way he saw Pete sitting in a boat out on the lake. He looked at the island, thinking of everything he'd recounted. He could see himself and Jamie standing at the top of the hill on the shore, him running back from the screams and paddling toward the boat. He could see his father zooming across the cove in a motorboat, frantically trying to get to his children.

The images that were strongest in his mind were the ones of him forcing his brother to go down the trail, the reason his entire family was killed. The thought of it was simply too heavy of a burden for him to bear.

When he got back to the lodge, Felix was nowhere in sight. All of the firefighters had left, as well as the sheriff. He appeared to be alone in the lodge. He walked behind the bar and started grabbing liquor bottles at random. He yanked the tops off each one and poured the liquor down without regard for himself or anything else around. He drank and drank until he finally stumbled to his room and passed out on the floor.

— — —

A hazy dream came to him. He was once again in front of the cabin. But this time he had no sense of self; he could only see and hear a specific vision ahead. The path in front of him was empty and yet the horrible creaking noises shrieked out of the buckling wooden steps leading up to the porch, one by one, produced from some invisible force. Footsteps rained across the porch, leading to the door. The door crept open by itself and it gave way to that infinite, unknowable blackness behind it.

And now there was something very different coming from it: it was a terrible laughter, produced from a being of great malice. The laugh beckoned him to come forth and step into the dreadful dark.

It was Nathaniel, the Black Warden.

— CHAPTER FIFTEEN —

PETE GOES MISSING

Mark opened his eyes.

"Mark!" Felix repeated, his eyes wide with panic. "Wake up!" He grabbed him by the shoulders and shook him.

It took a few seconds for Mark to understand where he was. "Wha?" he grumbled.

"It's Pete!" Felix said. "He's missing. I can't find him anywhere!"

Mark pushed himself up into a sitting position on the soft surface under him. He was sitting on the bed in his room. He didn't remember crawling onto it, but he was glad he wasn't still on the floor. It would be one less thing to explain to Felix, anyway. Not that he wanted to explain anything right now. He was still extremely drunk and it took all the energy he had to look at Felix while he talked.

Felix seemed too distracted to notice this as he began to recount all the places where he searched for Pete.

"Okay," Mark said. He had a nagging feeling that there was something else he should have said, but his brain couldn't connect the dots.

"His boat's still sitting out in the middle of the lake," Felix continued. "It's like he got out and swam away or something. But I just called the police and I'm going to do another sweep in and around the lodge until they get here. I need you to take a look around the grounds as well, and go talk to Hector... find out if he saw anything. You've got a quicker foot than I do, but just make sure you don't go too far into the woods." He shot Mark a concerned glance, thinking about the night before. And with that, he turned and hurried out of the room.

Mark was left sitting on his bed, trying to understand what happened to him before he passed out. The memories lingered on the edge of his mind, but they were shrouded by his drunkenness. They remained as fuzzy thoughts that taunted him, but after a few seconds he couldn't even remember what he was thinking about.

He fell back onto the bed and lay there for what seemed like hours, though in his warped sense of mind it was probably only a few minutes.

A strong urge rose up from deep within him, forcing him to get up. A stinging sensation rose up his throat and he leaned forward on the bed and puked on the floor. He felt a little better after that. His head had a dull ache to it, but he was still able to get up.

With shaky arms, he pushed himself onto his feet and took care not to step in his vomit as he stumbled toward the open doorway. When he got there, he put his hands on either side of the doorframe to brace himself as he looked down the hallway in both directions.

No sign of Pete there, he thought with a giddy, dream-like smile. He turned left and walked down the hallway, remarking aloud to himself that he'd never been this way before. He poked his head in each of the empty guest rooms, occasionally forgetting where he was or why he was there. Eventually, he made his way out to the lounge. He glanced out the window and saw Pete's boat sitting on the lake. Dark clouds had formed in the sky and a steady rain poured down across the land.

He shoved himself through the lounge doors and headed for the lake. The gravel path leading down to the docks looked steeper than he remembered. Not wanting to tumble down, he sat on the ground and slowly crawled down the path. As he did, images of his brother climbing down the trail floated through his head.

When he got to the bottom, he made his way to a motorboat sitting at the end of one of the docks. He lost his balance and fell into it. The boat rocked violently in the water and he groaned at some distant pain that was harping at him. A layer of ashy, gray dirt lined the boat's floor. He pushed himself up and brushed the dirt off his clothes without taking note of it. Then he untied the knot holding the boat to the dock then twisted around to prime the motor. He grabbed the cord and swung his arm in a wild jerk, yanking it at an odd angle. The motor sputtered a couple of times, but it didn't catch. He put his other hand on the top of it and gave the cord another few pulls. Finally, the motor caught and chugged into life.

His feelings of drunkenness suddenly disappeared and a new feeling filled his head. It was a strange tingling that he'd never experienced before. The feeling was so deep that it felt like it was invading his consciousness, influencing how he thought. He shook his head, trying to get rid of the frightening feeling, but it remained, slowly sinking its hooks deeper into his brain.

He looked out over the lake, scanning for any sign of Pete. Aside from the rain splashing across its surface, the water was calm. Pete's boat looked empty outside of a fishing pole that was propped up inside.

Then Mark saw him.

A head bobbed up from the surface of the water, followed by the burly torso that it was connected to. The body floated facedown in the water.

Mark's heart stopped and he tried to utter Pete's name, but nothing came out. He set off toward him, trying to keep his hand as steady as possible as he steered the boat toward the body.

The tingling feeling in his head became very strong, wrapping around his brain like a boa constrictor. His head itched from the inside, and he scraped his fingernails along the spot, frantically trying to scratch it. The feeling was maddening. Paranoid thoughts began to creep up in his mind. He started to look all around him, always thinking that someone was right behind him.

A HAUNTING AT HOLLOW'S COVE

He reached Pete and pulled the boat to a stop, leaning over the edge to see if he was still alive. But Pete's skin was already turning white. Mark fought the terrible feeling gnawing at his sanity as he reached into the water and pulled Pete's body into the boat. It was incredibly heavy and Mark struggled as it slowly slid over the lip of the boat like a slippery fish. Pete fell inside and Mark turned him over.

It wasn't Pete.

Mark looked in horror as a pale white face, rotting and bloated with water, stared up at him. The body was naked and devoid of any gender; it was a hideous, vague corpse that looked like it was dredged up from Hell itself. Its flesh was slimy and looked as if it had started to peel, revealing a network of black veins underneath. The nappy hair coming out of its head was caked with a disgusting grime. The flesh on its fingers was peeled down to discolored bone. Its eyes were picked clean, leaving black holes in its skull. Its teeth were bared, each blackened, diseased tooth jutting crookedly out of its face.

He shrunk away from the ghastly figure. A coldness wrapped around his ankle. As he looked down, he saw those bony, yellowed fingers gripped tightly on his leg. With slow realization, his gaze traced along the corpse's arm up to its face. The face was looking at him. There were no eyes, but it could see.

The corpse kept its dead gaze on him as it pulled itself toward him. Its fingers scraped against the floor of the boat, producing a nauseating sound. Its jaw slung low and revealed the blackness at the back of its throat. As it came closer, it snapped its jaw shut, its teeth crashing and grinding together.

Mark pushed himself to the back of the boat, as far away as he could get. He desperately tried to shake the corpse's hand off his ankle as the icy grip got tighter and tighter. The itching feeling in his head got worse. It felt like there was a colony of bugs burrowing through his brain.

He finally wrestled his foot away from the bloated corpse and hiked his legs up to his body. As the ghoul got closer, he kicked at it. Its wet body slipped around the boat, struggling to grab hold of Mark. Each blow knocked it farther back. The itch in Mark's head became unbearable and he ground his teeth together as he frantically kicked at the monstrosity in front of him. With another hard strike, the corpse teetered over the edge of the boat and fell into the water.

Mark lay on his back, stretched out in the boat. He was exhausted and closed his eyes. His head swam, and that damn itching feeling wouldn't go away. But for a moment, everything was calm.

A bubble rose to the surface of the water and popped.

Mark's eyes opened.

Ripples broke out on the surface all around him. He peered over the edge of the boat and gasped. Pale white corpses rose up all around him. They climbed into the boat from every direction. Mark fought off their slimy grips, but he was soon overwhelmed. They pinned him down and his face was pressed against the ashy dirt. A dozen black eye sockets stared at him as they pulled him overboard. Mark screamed, but soon they were pushing his head underwater and his lungs filled with the lake's black, icy contents.

His head bobbed above the surface for a moment and he caught a glimpse of the island. It had morphed into a giant, blackened skull. Frightening fires blazed in its hollow eye sockets. The whole land mass turned in the water and looked directly at him, then opened its gigantic jaw and began sailing toward him to swallow him whole. Its open mouth cut through the water, sending black waves crashing to each side.

Then the monolithic skull consumed him, delivering black death.

— CHAPTER SIXTEEN —

Pete Goes Bananas

When Mark regained consciousness, Felix, Jerry and Hector were standing over him. He dumbly blinked at them and started to groan. A terrible migraine pounded through his head, like his brain was continually ramming into the inside of his skull.

"How you feeling?" Felix asked.

"Kill me," Mark replied.

Felix laughed, but Jerry and Hector looked uneasy.

It was clear to Mark that he was lying on the floor and he could see just enough of the room around him to know that he was in the lounge. The sound of heavy rain slapping the exterior of the lodge echoed throughout the otherwise silent room. The sky outside had turned to night and the only lights on in the lodge were the ones in the lounge; the rest of the place sat in an eerie darkness.

"What time is it?" Mark asked.

Jerry looked at his gold watch. "It's just about midnight."

The drunkenness was gone and was replaced by what could be called clarity of mind if it weren't for his splitting migraine. Even still, he had the mental capacity to remember the day's events. They all came trickling into his brain, one at a time.

"Where's Pete?" Mark asked.

The three men standing over him suddenly looked sad and turned their heads away.

"We don't know," Felix admitted. "We still can't find him. Police looked all over the grounds and in the lake, but he didn't turn up."

Mark was about to say something, but stopped. He moved his body and felt that the only thing between him and the hard floor was a thin blanket. "Why am I on the floor?"

"Because when we tried to move you to the bed," Felix said, "you refused, saying the floor was where you belonged."

Mark groaned again and squeezed his eyes shut, pressing a hand to his forehead. "Well I've changed my mind; I think I've decided the floor isn't the place for me after all."

Felix chuckled then bent to help him up. Jerry helped too, and they began to hoist him onto his feet.

"Slowly, slowly!" Mark protested. When he was on his feet, he stumbled to the bar with Felix and Jerry's help. They eased him onto a stool and he leaned forward against the bar top. "Don't suppose you've got anything for this earthquake in my head, do you?"

Felix walked around the bar. "Course I do." He poured some water into a glass and fished a couple of Tylenol tablets out of a bottle. He slid them across the bar and Mark graciously took them.

Hector and Jerry pulled up stools beside him. Hector leaned forward and traced lines in the wooden bar top with his finger. "I know it was a lot to take in today," he said to Mark, "but I didn't think you'd take it this hard. I certainly didn't want you to feel bad about what happened."

Mark nodded. "Don't worry about it." Embarrassment fell over him, knowing he would probably have to explain to Felix and Jerry what Hector was talking about. But silence held in the air and he looked up to see that Felix and Jerry didn't have any confusion on their faces.

"I take it you told them?" Mark asked Hector.

"I did."

"It's hard to believe you're that little boy from so long ago," Felix said. "I had no idea."

"So what do you make of it all, Felix?" Mark asked. "Do you think those boys up in the woods are behind all this?"

Felix considered this for a long while. "That's the impression I'm getting," he said. "I really can't see it any other way."

Mark cupped his hands and rested his head on them. His migraine had only subsided a tiny bit. After a few moments, he lifted his head again.

"Do you think they have Pete?" he asked.

All eyes in the room darted to him and everyone held a scared look. It was something that every one of them thought, but was too afraid to say out loud. When no one said anything, Mark continued.

"Assuming Pete knows his way around a fishing pond," he said, "and assuming he wasn't any drunker today than I was, there's no way he would have simply fallen off his boat. And when I went out there, I—" He trailed off and stayed quiet, suddenly without the urge to continue his thought. He vividly remembered the nightmarish corpses that he fought off on that boat, and the terrible skull-island that sailed at him. It felt so real to him at the time, but it had all just been a hallucination.

"What *did* happen out there?" Felix asked.

"I don't know," Mark said. "I got to Pete's boat, then I... I just fell. That's the last thing that I remember."

"Well, in any case, count yourself lucky," Felix said. "If I hadn't seen you in time, you would've been fish food. Hector helped me drag you in here. You woke up just enough to cough up all the water in your lungs, then you passed out again until now." Felix walked around the bar and sat on the last stool next to the other three. He reached into his pocket and pulled out a toothpick.

"Pete said he was going to get some fishing in before the storm hit," he said, nibbling on the toothpick. "That's the last time I saw him." His face turned glum as he reflected on his last sentence. "By the way, the window in the library's already been replaced. Figured a tarp wouldn't do when this storm hits."

A swell of rain picked up and pounded on the lodge as the four of them sat in silence, staring blankly in various directions. They listened to the howling wind squeezing through the cracks in the building.

The doors beside the bar burst open and Pete barreled through. No one could even turn their head to look at him in time before he was already upon them. He dove into Felix and sent him crashing into Jerry, who in turn knocked over Hector and Mark like dominoes. All of them tipped over and fell to the ground with hard thuds.

Pete straddled Felix and viciously hammered on his chest with his meaty fists. He looked like he had just been dragged through a swamp; his clothes were soaked and dirty, his hair matted and caked with grime. He ground his teeth with each strike, spit flying from the corners of his mouth. His face was contorted into an almost caricature-like display of rage.

Felix's eyes glazed over as each savage hit pounded the air out of him. Jerry got to his feet and yelled at Pete to stop. Without a moment's notice, Pete directed his malice at Jerry and lunged at him, taking out his legs and almost making his body do a flip before slamming on the floor. Pete crouched over top of Jerry's crumpled body and began taking large swipes at his face, clawing flesh off with each swing.

Mark tried to tackle Pete, but he redirected him with a strong blow to the head. Mark flew head-first into one of the pool table's legs. Intense pain ripped through his skull and left him temporarily immobile.

Jerry desperately tried to shield his face from Pete's swipes, but Pete's abnormally strong arms knocked his hands away. Pete bent over and started biting his neck, tearing flesh away like a hungry wolf.

Mark was in pure agony, but he fought through the pain and got back on his feet. He jumped on Pete's back and wrapped his arms around his throat, wrestling him off of Jerry. Seemingly without effort, Pete stood up with Mark hanging on him and charged backward, smashing him into the wall. Mark slumped to the floor, gasping for breath.

Pete turned his gaze to the only person he hadn't savaged: Hector. He slowly walked toward him, Jerry's blood seeping out of his mouth. Hector was terrified, holding his hands out in front of him as if it would deter him. He slowly walked backward with shaky legs, trying to get away from him, but not knowing where to go. His heel caught on one of the overturned barstools and he fell to the ground. An expression of complete disbelief washed over his face as he frantically scrambled backward on the floor, away from Pete's looming figure. All at once, Pete's muscles jerked into motion and he charged toward Hector.

A deafening shotgun blast rang out. Pete's body sailed forward and crashed to the floor, inches away from Hector. Hector began to tremble as he stared wide-eyed at Pete's dead body in front of him. He couldn't hold it in anymore: his bladder gave way and a dark spot formed on the seam of his pants.

Felix stood behind the bar, aiming his shotgun where Pete used to be. He dropped it onto the bar then collapsed on it. His face was pale and he gasped for breath, a thick wheezing sound rattling in and out of his lungs. Mark started to get to his feet. He held his chest and took deep breaths. Jerry was still lying on the floor, shaking and bleeding profusely. Mark fell to his knees beside him and pressed his hands to his wound. Felix grabbed the first aid kit and tossed it to him.

"Hector!" Felix yelled, his head pressed against the bar top.

Hector was still sitting on the floor, frozen in shock. Felix's call snapped him out of his trance and he looked around the room. When he spotted Jerry, he clambered across the floor to him. Hector picked up the first aid kit and pulled out most of its contents. He gently moved Mark's hands away from the wound and went to work on it. Mark fell back against the leg of the pool table and placed a hand on his head. Felix reached over and picked up the phone, clumsily punching numbers into the keypad.

Mark felt like his head was being squeezed in a vice grip. Pain rippled through it in waves. The light in the room was too bright for him, sending sharp pain directly to his brain. He looked at the window overlooking the lake.

Out in the darkness, Cleaver stood there, staring into the lounge.

Mark did a double-take and he and Cleaver maintained a shocked stare with each other for a moment. Cleaver turned and took off, running toward his house as fast as he could. Without missing a beat, Mark launched himself up and took off after him. He grabbed Felix's shotgun as he passed the bar, then he hurdled himself through the doors and out into the rainy night.

Cleaver sprinted along the lodge, heading toward the woods. Mark followed, trying not to slip on the rain-slicked gravel. He was slowly gaining on him. There was no way Cleaver could make it anywhere close to his house before he got to him.

Cleaver passed the corner of the lodge and began his ascent up the hill. Mark was closing in now. He was almost at the corner himself.

Just as he approached it, a tall figure stepped out from around the other side. The last thing Mark saw was the blurry sight of a two-by-four swinging across his field of vision. The end came to him with blackness and a sickening whack.

— CHAPTER SEVENTEEN —

IN THE PRESENCE OF DEATH

Mark could feel himself inside some kind of container as it was dragged, rattling over bumps in the ground. He groaned in pain as his body rolled around inside. It felt rough, like it was made of wood, and there was a terrible smell of metal to it. The scent was very familiar, but he didn't want to admit what it was. Rain pattered the top of the container over his head and he could faintly hear footsteps on either side of him. A series of rough grunts happened on both sides, sounding almost like his two captors were carrying on a conversation. It was very close to being language, but it sounded like both men had something caught in their throats, unable to properly pronounce the words. His container moved in heaves and he could tell that he was going uphill.

He squeezed an arm around in the tight container and touched his head. Pain exploded in it and he quickly brought his arm back down. He tried to remember what happened to him, but everything was fuzzy.

Eventually, the dragging stopped and he felt his container tilt upright. There was a momentary pause then he was tipped again and heaved upward. He was being pulled up a set of stairs, his container banging into each one as it went up. He was set upright again when he got to the top, and the two men made their way across what sounded like the creaking wood of a porch. There was a jangling of keys followed by one of them being jammed into a lock and turned. A door opened slowly and stopped partway. More footsteps, a pause, then the sound of the door opening the rest of the way.

This was the moment when Mark realized where he was being taken: the brothers' house—the dilapidated house of boarded-up windows, through which only the screams of the dying escape.

When this realization set in, the strangely familiar smell in his container that he tried not to think about was painfully obvious now: it was blood.

His body froze, rigid with fear, as his container tipped again. He placed his hands against the front of the container and pushed, as if trying to keep himself from entering the house. His container scraped across the floor with a painful slowness as he was dragged inside—into the very presence of death.

The door slammed shut behind him. The sounds of the rain and wind were still very audible, giving credence to the age and disrepair of the house. A sudden crack of thunder penetrated it and echoed all around. A tiny bead of light fell on Mark's face and he pressed his eye to the hole in the container where it shone through. He managed to catch a glimpse of a wide staircase in the entrance leading up to the second floor just before he was dragged down a long hallway. At the end of it, he was pulled around a corner and set upright. There was a violent shove and his equilibrium fell into total confusion. For the briefest moment, he felt like he was floating in nothingness. Then there was an incredible crash that shook his body as it rebounded against the walls of the container in accompaniment to a sharp, splintering sound. His head whipped and smashed against what was now the floor of the container. Tremendous pain rattled in his head, crippling his body.

The footsteps turned and left. As they faded down the long hallway, Mark could hear the men grunt again before they were out of earshot. He lay on his stomach with his body twisted at a painful angle in his tiny confinements. He squeezed his eyelids shut, trying to quell the pain coursing through his head. Slowly it subsided and he managed to flip himself onto his back.

There was a crack in the top of the wooden container and he could see flickering orange light painting the walls through it. In the faint light, he could see that the top of the container was a lid that was nailed to the frame.

The smell of blood overcame him again, stronger than before. He started to become nauseous and he pushed on the lid. It came apart slightly from the rest of the frame and he pushed on it with both hands enough to wedge one of his knees under it. He shoved it with all of his might until it splintered and broke off from the frame. The lid flipped over and hit the wall beside it. His heart skipped a beat, worried that someone might have heard it, and he climbed out of his wooden box and looked around. He was in a walk-in closet. There was a hole in the wall where the plaster had been chipped away and the old boards beneath had been removed. The orange light was coming through the hole from candles in a large living room on the other side of the hallway. There was no sign of anyone around. He looked around the rest of the closet then he turned and saw the container he'd been kept in.

It was a coffin. He figured that it didn't matter what it was, but all the same he couldn't help an icy feeling that crawled across his skin.

Footsteps echoed down the hallway. Panic swept over him. Someone *did* hear him break out. He glanced at the coffin with its fractured lid lying next to it and hopelessness set in, knowing that he was trapped. His only chance was to hide and make it look like he escaped.

There were a few dusty, crumbling sheets of plaster propped against the corner of the room. He slipped behind them and constricted his body as much as he could, making sure he was entirely hidden. He waited and listened as the footsteps grew louder and louder. He closed his eyes tightly and held his breath, knowing it was his last.

The footsteps reached the end of the hallway and turned. He felt himself tense as they stopped. He waited, praying that the man would go away. A long moment passed in silence. Knowing it was a mistake, but not being able to help himself, he poked his head out from behind the plaster sheets.

There was no one in the closet.

The sound of old fabric being stretched came from the living room across the hall. Mark peeked through the hole in the wall and saw a decrepit armchair facing away from him with the back of someone's head propped up just over the top of it. He recognized the scraggly hair from the day before when he saw the brothers pull up to their house. It was Firebug. He sat in the flickering light, spinning a lighter on a dirty chairside table next to him.

The rain outside battered the house with enough force to drown out most of the noise inside. It waxed and waned in uneven intervals with the fickle wind. Between the barrages, Mark could hear the footsteps of Hunter and Cleaver walking back and forth on the floor above. If they were upstairs, then there was no one guarding the front door. All he had to do was sneak past Firebug and he'd be home free.

He waited for each volley of rain as he stepped out into the hallway. He crept along the wall, trying to step on the edges of the floorboards where they would make less noise. As he went, he kept his eyes locked on the back of Firebug's head. There was something very odd about him just sitting there, staring at the wall. It was like he was waiting for something.

A HAUNTING AT HOLLOW'S COVE

Mark waited for the next heavy volley of rain to wash over the house, but it didn't come. It almost sounded like it was starting to clear up outside. He froze with his foot hanging in the air. An eerie silence fell over the house and he could clearly hear the metal of Firebug's lighter spinning on the wooden table. He braced himself against the wall and tried not to shift his weight, but he still couldn't help the minute squeaks of the floorboards under him. His heart hammered faster and faster. The rain still didn't pick up. He was standing in plain sight; all Firebug had to do was turn his head and it would all be over.

His leg became increasingly more tired as he supported his weight on it. It soon began to wobble and the quiet squeaks from the floorboards became more frequent. The scratching of Firebug's lighter on the table grated on his nerves. It was deafening in the horrible silence.

Hunter and Cleaver suddenly changed direction upstairs. They were headed toward the front of the house. Toward the stairs.

An icy feeling clutched Mark's spine and he morbidly wondered if that was the Grim Reaper's hand wrapped around it.

When the footsteps above almost reached the stairs, they turned and traveled to another room.

Mark let out a silent sigh of relief and before he realized what he was doing, he took a step toward the entrance of the house. An achingly loud creak screamed out of the floorboards under his foot. He gasped and spun his head toward Firebug.

Firebug stopped spinning his lighter right on cue. He looked like he'd been frozen as well. His gangly fingers pressed on top of the lighter's surface as he stared forward, then his head perked up and cocked to the side, listening. He shifted in his chair and turned his ear to the direction of the sound, his head only a small turn away from seeing Mark.

Just then, the rain began to pick up again. A sudden gust of wind howled and forced itself into the cracks of the house, thundering down the empty hallways. The rain came down heavily, drowning out the silence. After another moment, Firebug finally turned his head back toward the living room and resumed twirling his lighter.

Mark felt a prickling sensation all over his skin and he desperately wanted to be out of sight. He continued down the hallway as quickly as the covering wind and rain permitted. He reached the dark entrance of the house, and the only light coming in was the moonlight through the thin cracks between the boards covering two tall windows on either side of the front door. He moved toward the door and froze when he saw what was in front of it: a shotgun was mounted on a makeshift wooden stand, pointed at the doorway. A long piece of wire was attached at one end to the trigger of the shotgun. He traced the wire with his eyes as it went through a series of rings, finally stretching across the bottom of the door and ending at a ring sitting on a hook screwed into the frame.

The trap that Felix told him about, set in this very doorway all those years ago, came into his mind: that swinging blade that dug into his knee, shattering it. It was designed to activate when the door was opened, probably in this very same way. It seemed the brothers wanted to keep all intruders out of their house, even if that meant openly murdering someone.

Mark carefully looked at the trap. The concept seemed primitive enough, and all he had to do was disarm it and walk out the door. He approached the mounted shotgun as quietly as he could and inspected the wire tied to the trigger. He looked at the other end that was hooked next to the door. The wire was loose, giving room for the door to be opened about halfway before the shotgun would go off. He crouched down and carefully pulled the ringed end of the wire off the hook by the door. Now he wouldn't trigger it when he opened the door. He backed away and stood up, surveying the area until he was satisfied that all he had to do was open the door and leave. It seemed too good to be true. As he moved to the door, he glanced over his shoulder at the shotgun pointing in his direction, wondering with morose irony if it would somehow go off. He grabbed the deadbolt and turned it.

There, unlocked.

He turned the doorknob then gave it a firm tug.

It didn't budge.

He pulled again, but the door held firmly in place. Getting frantic now, he grabbed the deadbolt and turned it in each direction, wrenching on the door as he did it. Utter confusion fell over him as he struggled to understand how this was happening. He did everything he needed to do, but still the door wouldn't open. He savagely yanked on the doorknob in frustration, then he saw the reason it remained shut.

There was a second deadbolt in the door, a ways above the one he unlocked. But this one was reversed, with the keyhole facing him; the brothers didn't only want to keep people out, they wanted to keep people *in*.

His heart sank. He wondered with grim defeat how many prisoners before him had gotten to the door only to realize that there was no escape for them.

Quick footsteps sounded from somewhere upstairs. He spun around and looked at the staircase leading to the upper floor. There was no mistaking that someone heard him trying to open the door. Someone was coming for him.

— CHAPTER EIGHTEEN —

Trapped

Panic stiffened his muscles as he tried to decide what to do. He reached for the shotgun and attempted to pull it off the stand, but it was somehow stuck to it. He glanced around the entrance of the house for a hiding spot and saw a dark closet sitting next to the staircase.

The door! he thought.

He turned the deadbolt back to the side to lock it, then bent down and fumbled with the ring as he tried to put it back on the hook. He concentrated very hard so he wouldn't yank on the wire and blow his brains out, but his hands were shaking badly.

The footsteps sounded like they were in the hallway above, almost at the stairs.

Out of blind panic, Mark took one last swipe to put the ring back on the hook, but he missed it. Knowing there was no time, he scurried over to the closet beside the staircase.

Almost immediately after he reached the closet and stowed himself away in its darkest corner, the heavy sounds of footsteps rained down the stairs beside him. He started to pull one of the closet's shuttered doors closed in front of him, but it let out a low whine as soon as he touched it. His hand snapped back from it as if it had just bitten him.

Cleaver stood in the entrance of the house. His head was cocked in a peculiar direction as if he were listening for any betraying sounds. He turned his attention to the door and cautiously walked over to it, inspecting the doorknob and locks. He moved to one of the windows and stuck his face up to the boards covering it. After a few moments, he stepped back in front of the door. He looked at the locks and doorknob again and turned each one, making sure they were secure.

The wire was lying on the floor, undone. If Cleaver looked down and saw it, he would know the noise didn't come from outside.

Mark patted his hand on the floor around him, trying to find anything that he could defend himself with. His hand came over a small shard of wood. It wasn't much, but it was all he had.

Cleaver stood over the wire, staring ahead in space as if something weren't right.

Mark's fingers tightened around the splintered wood.

The coalescence of rain and wind battered the house. It was the only sound in the otherwise silent standoff.

Cleaver turned and casually swung his head around the room. For a horrifying moment, his eyes flashed where Mark was hiding. He paused, staring at the darkened closet. Mark's eyes went wide and he held the piece of wood with an iron grip, ready but terrified. Cleaver looked away and started up the stairs. Mark let out a stilted breath.

Did he see me? he thought. The idea was nauseating, and worse yet, maybe Cleaver went upstairs to fetch Hunter.

Mark crawled out of the closet and continued around a corner and into the dining room. It was almost pitch-black with no windows to illuminate anything. Beyond it was the kitchen, which had some faint light coming through a boarded window just above the sink. He paused and listened for the footsteps overhead. He heard Cleaver return to a room at the far end of the house. After waiting a few more moments, the footsteps ended there.

The kitchen was the messiest area Mark had seen so far. The countertops were covered in old dishes and bits of food. Various parts of chickens were torn and scattered across the room without any apparent regard. Some of the animal carcasses were strewn onto the floor or slopped across the stove. Occasionally a pig leg could be seen mixed in with the chicken bits, and there were a few pieces of meat that he wasn't convinced came from an animal. The room reeked of blood and garbage. The floor was stained all over with various dark splotches. Some appeared that they'd been there so long that they turned black.

An ancient and unpowered refrigerator was butted up against the wall separating the kitchen and the dining room. Its door was streaked with long-dried liquids and sat ajar, allowing a glimpse inside the darkened, mostly empty fridge. Judging by how long the brothers appeared to be living without electricity, Mark wondered if this fridge ever saw use as anything other than a very heavy cabinet. Its shelves and drawers had been removed, leaving nothing inside but a garbage pile.

Mark looked at the boarded window above the sink, wondering if he should try to make his escape through it. All three of the brothers seemed to be in faraway parts of the house, leaving him time to pry some of the boards off. He took a step toward the window then faltered. Even if he could somehow remove them silently, there was no guarantee that the window wasn't simply bolted shut. He would need to break through it, and he didn't think he would get very far in the woods before Hunter tracked him down.

The only other exit point was a door in the back corner of the kitchen. On his way to investigate it, he glanced over his shoulder at the dining room.

Someone was watching him. A silhouette leaned against the wall between the entrance and the dining room. In the dimness, a flash of eyes shone through, staring at him.

Mark drew himself behind the wall next to the fridge.

It was Cleaver; he'd just gone to get his axe before coming in for the kill. Or maybe it was Firebug, finally having checked on the coffin, only to find him gone.

There was no chance of escape. Mark clung onto the hope that he hadn't actually been seen. He glanced at the door in the corner of the kitchen, but he wouldn't be able to get to it without being seen. He had another idea. He originally dismissed it, but it was all he had. He opened the refrigerator door and climbed in as quietly as he could, shutting it silently. An incredible smell hit him, nearly making him throw up. It was the smell of months worth of putrid waste buildup. He pinched his nose and waited in agonizing silence.

There was a loud bang from outside as if the head of an axe had been dropped to the floor. Floorboards groaned, slowly leading to the kitchen.

Mark had no escape, and the only thing left to do was fight. The noises ended in front of the fridge. Mark clenched his fist in terror. The door was yanked open. Mark lunged forward, ready to strike. But there was no one there. After a moment of confusion, he looked down and saw who opened the door.

It wasn't Cleaver or Firebug. It was a man lying on the floor. He looked up at Mark, his face very gaunt and severely beaten. Mark had never seen a more desperate look in someone's eyes before. It was the look of someone pleading for help with what little life he had left. The man reached for him and Mark could see that three of his fingers were severed. He opened his mouth as if to let out a cry, but no sound came out.

Footsteps sounded from overhead again. They headed toward the stairs and quickly galloped down.

Mark's heart raced as he listened to the footsteps rounding the corner into the dining room. He tried to pull the fridge door shut again, but the man threw his arm in the way and kept it open. The man looked at him with the same pleading eyes.

"*I can't help you!*" Mark whispered.

Tears streamed down the man's face as he looked up at Mark, his hand still outstretched for help. It was the most heartbreaking thing Mark had ever witnessed.

"*I can't help you!*" he repeated, trying to move the man's arm out of the way. "*I'm sorry! I'm sorry!*"

The man was suddenly dragged out of view toward the dining room, his mangled hand the last thing that Mark saw. A new arm grabbed the refrigerator door and slammed it shut.

Mark listened with bated breath. Footsteps headed to the dining room, followed by something that sounded like an axe being buried into a wet tree stump. A garbled cry, and then silence. The footsteps returned to the entrance and bounded up the stairs, leaving Mark alone.

He burst out of the refrigerator and fell on all fours. He panted and forced himself not to throw up. Mark wiped his mouth with his sleeve and got to his feet. He staggered to the closed door in the corner of the kitchen and opened it, praying that it would lead to a way out.

A horrid stench was the first thing that met him. But it wasn't like the stench from the fridge; this smelled more of very old decay. Beyond the door, a few steps went down to a landing connected to a flight of stairs leading down into darkness.

It wasn't a way out; it was the basement. But he didn't know where else he could go. His only option was to go down and hope that there was a window he could sneak out of, far enough away from the brothers in case he had to break through the glass.

He walked down onto the landing and closed the door behind him. Complete darkness covered him. He knew he had to move quickly, as the evidence of his escape was piling up behind him, but he had no idea what was at the bottom of the stairs; there could have been another trap for all he knew.

His hand slipped into his pocket and touched his wallet. His fingers nervously worked their way into the folds as he stared into the darkness and decided what to do. He felt a small folded object inside. He remembered now: the matchbook he took when he checked in at Hollow's Cove.

Mark pulled out a match and swiped it against the matchbook's striker strip. A small orange flame burst into life. It gave faint illumination of the immediate area, but nothing more. The door that he'd just gone through had metal hooks screwed into the frame on either side. A steel rod was propped in the corner of the landing. He picked it up and wedged it into the metal hooks, barring the door.

Just in case I need to buy some time, he thought.

The glow of the match's light only lit the first few steps on the staircase in front of him. But Mark descended them, venturing headlong into the dark. The potent smell of must and decay became stronger. The noise of the rain, sounding a little more detached, droned on in the background. Aside from it, there was an uneasy silence that permeated the room. He felt like something unsavory was waiting for him, waiting for anyone to come down and discover it. And when he reached the bottom of the stairs and took a step on what should have been cement, he understood.

It was something brittle. It crumbled under his foot as his weight came down on it. He crouched and held the match over the floor. In the flame's limited light, a large pile of bones could be seen on the floor around him, and they looked too large to be from chickens or pigs. He swept the flame to his right and saw a skull peeking out from under an assorted pile of bones. It was unmistakably human.

"...my God," he uttered.

He swept the match in a wide arc over the floor. The entire basement, as far as he could see, was filled with human remains. He pressed a hand to his queasy stomach and leaned against the wall to steady himself.

Felix was right. He'd been right the whole time and no one believed him. No one bought a word of what he said as the bodies piled up.

A hot ball of emotion rested in Mark's stomach. It was an amalgam of disgust, hatred and sadness. He felt lightheaded. His head still throbbed from all the trauma he'd taken earlier, but it felt a little better now. He glanced around the room and saw that there were no windows, unless they'd been completely covered. Yet there was an odd pattering of rain from somewhere in the darkness that was louder than from any other direction.

He slowly walked along the wall beside him, crunching old bones underfoot. With each step, he felt a twinge of guilt, like he was desecrating the already desecrated dead. He came upon an old wooden dresser sitting against the wall. A number of dusty candles sat on its surface. He picked one up and blew the dust off of it, then held the match's flame to the wick. The flame jumped to the candle, helping to light the darkness around him. He lit the others then went back and placed one on the edge of the stairs. He shook out his match and tossed it away, then picked up another lit candle from the dresser and took it with him as he carefully stepped over the bones toward the sound of the rain. The candle's light cut through the darkness to reveal a staircase that led up to a set of cellar doors. He could clearly hear the rain splashing on the other side of it.

His heart gave a leap of excitement. As he headed for the stairs, he bumped into something situated just in front of them. It was another shotgun fastened to a stand, pointing up at the cellar doors. Just like the other one, a wire stretched from the trigger of the gun to a hook screwed into one of the doors. He carefully made his way up the stairs and unhooked the ring attached to the end of the wire, unthreading it through a large ring attached to the second door. With the trap disarmed, he gave a gentle push on the cellar doors. Locked. He pushed the doors open as far as they would go and through the crack he saw a padlock on the other side.

Mark's heart bottomed out. Had he come so close to escape only to be foiled yet again? He glanced down at the shotgun. It looked like it was pointing approximately where the lock was. His heartbeat quickened and he licked his dry lips in anticipation of what he was about to do.

He went down the stairs and crouched behind the stand, looking along the gun's line of sight. It was just about dead center to the padlock.

He paused, a sudden apprehension to what he was thinking coming over him. If he was going to do this, he only had one shot. And even then, the metal rod he barred the door with would buy him some time when the brothers heard the shot, but only until they realized where he was; then they would go around the outside of the house and cut him off. How far would he really get before they hunted him down? He carefully tugged on the shotgun to see if it would come loose; he would use it on the brothers if he could. But it was somehow fastened to the stand.

He let out a frustrated sigh. No matter how he thought about it, there was just no escaping. He moved toward the far end of the basement, looking for anything else that could help him. Sitting against the back wall was a very large fuel tank, a few shelves and a tarnished oven. He paused when he got to the oven. There was a hose connected to the top of it that led to the fuel tank. Everything looked like it hadn't been touched in ages, and he wondered if there was any gas left in the tank. He looked down at the candle in his hand, mesmerized by its flame.

It was crazy. He couldn't believe he was even thinking about it. But it was his only chance. He went back to the stairs leading up to the cellar doors and placed the candle on it. It offered enough light to faintly illuminate the fuel tank and the oven. He moved back to the oven and unscrewed the hose, laying it out over the floor. He walked to the tank and rested his hand on the valve. He looked toward the shotgun and the cellar doors one more time to make sure he knew what he had to do. He took a deep breath then turned the valve. The hiss of gas seeped out of the hose. He ran over to the shotgun and pulled the trigger. An ear-shattering bang ripped and rebounded through the basement. Small chunks of wood in the cellar doors were shredded away, and rain poured through.

Almost immediately, distant but heavy footsteps whirred into a frenzy from far above.

Mark climbed the stairs quickly and shoved the doors, but they didn't open. He reached an arm through a small hole in one of them and felt the padlock on the other side. It was still intact; the buckshot missed.

"No," he said, his eyes wide. "No, no, *no!*" He climbed back down the stairs and crouched behind the shotgun. He pulled the trigger. An empty click was all that came from the gun. "No!" he yelled. He pulled the trigger again and again, but the result was the same.

The door leading to the basement from inside the house opened, knocking into the metal rod that barred it shut. The door slammed furiously against it and howling cries issued from the gap. A few seconds later, the sound of an axe cutting through the door rang down the stairs.

Mark turned and looked at the hose on the floor, still pumping its deadly gas into the room. He ran up the stairs to the cellar doors and threw everything he had into one of them. He rammed his shoulder repeatedly into the weakened wood, trying to break through it. A large chunk snapped off and left a hole almost big enough to escape. He wedged his body into it and wriggled it back and forth, trying to squeeze through. The only thought running through his head was that the gas could ignite at any second.

After what seemed like an agonizing eternity, he finally managed to slip an arm through the hole. He used all the strength in his legs to push off of the stairs below as he pulled himself out with his arm. The wood weakened then snapped and he was free. Mark shot out of the hole and sprinted around the corner of the house, finding himself at the side. As he headed for the lodge, he glanced over his shoulder.

The front door of the house was open and Hunter stood on the porch, staring at him.

A moment later, the entire house ripped apart in an enormous explosion. The incredibly loud sound cracked the sky and sent out a shockwave that knocked Mark off his feet. He rolled and skidded along the wet ground as a shard of wood stabbed into the front of his thigh. He let out a loud cry as pain coursed through his leg and into the rest of his body.

Thousands of pieces of debris rained from the sky, ravaging the trees all around. He forced himself to get out of the way as he clawed and dragged himself along the ground. He got to his feet again, against the protests of his leg, and limped as quickly as he could through the woods. He pulled the shard of wood out of his leg with a grunt and pressed a firm hand to the wound. His chest heaved shallowly, but he made himself continue without stopping. Every once in a while, he glanced over his shoulder to see if anyone was pursuing him, but no one was in sight.

When he made it out of the woods with the lodge in clear sight ahead, Felix was standing just outside of the lounge doors and hobbled over to him.

Mark lost his footing and tumbled the rest of the way down the hill. His head ached horribly and he took the opportunity to lie motionlessly on the ground.

"What the hell happened?!" Felix asked.

Mark was in no shape to talk. He remained on the ground, as still as possible. Felix saw the blood pouring from his thigh and began to help him inside.

— CHAPTER NINETEEN —

Looking Over the Wreckage

When Mark woke up in the morning, he could hear people outside talking to each other. He rolled over and slid himself out of bed, groaning at the pain that sprung up in various parts of his body. His aching head seemed to mostly subside over the course of his sleep, and the pain in his thigh from the shrapnel had turned into a dull throb. Felix patched him up when he got back to the lodge, but he didn't remember most of it.

He walked beside his bed and looked out the window.

Lots of firefighters meandered in and around the woods by the wreckage of the brothers' house. Mark put his face close to the glass and peeked around the corner to the left. There were a number of people standing about on the lodge grounds too, and he could just barely see Felix, talking to someone just out of sight.

He turned away from the window and walked into the bathroom. His leg tensed in pain with each step, but he tried to walk as normally as possible. He flicked on the light and leaned against the sink, staring at himself up and down in the mirror. For all the head trauma he took the day before, his face looked surprisingly normal; there was no bruising on his face, and there was only a small welt on his forehead from where the two-by-four hit him. He turned on the faucet and splashed water on his face. He dried off and walked to the lounge.

There was no sign of the scuffle that occurred the night before except for some blood on the floor that probably belonged to either Jerry or Pete. Mark heard the phantom sounds of the jukebox merrily playing in the background as the two of them sat at the bar and talked. Now they were gone: Pete, dead, and Jerry, unknown. He walked through the lounge doors.

Felix was talking with a deputy outside. He gave Mark a nod and continued his conversation. Mark nodded back and stood on the edge of the gravel path, looking at the wreckage of the brothers' house. The house that he destroyed. Thinking about it now, he could hardly believe that he did such a thing. The events of the night before seemed so far away and surreal. It felt like it was all just a strange dream. Yet here he was, looking over the wreckage that he created. The people he killed...

A tight knot rose up in his stomach. The people he killed. He never thought about it until just now, but he was technically a murderer. The people he murdered were better off dead, and in doing so, he probably saved countless lives, but still... there was something unsettling about what he did. He briefly wondered if his deeds would haunt him at some point in the future. For now, though, he tried to put it out of his mind.

Felix approached and stood beside him, staring at the wreckage as well.

"How's Jerry?" Mark asked.

"He took a bad lickin', but he should pull through just fine."

Relief washed over Mark. "And what about you?"

Felix laughed. "I'll be fine. It's you I'm more interested in." He paused, then said: "How did it feel?"

"What?"

"How did it feel to do it?"

Mark was silent.

Felix looked around to see if anyone was near them. "You never told me what happened last night. I see a house explode and you walking out of the wreckage... I'm going to assume that you did that. How you did it, I don't know. I just want to know how it felt to kill those bastards."

"Felix!"

Mark and Felix turned.

Clemington's sheriff, Hank Driscoll, stood at the top of the path. He gave a friendly wave and started down the slope.

"It felt like I was putting an end to a very bad thing," Mark said.

Felix studied him for a moment then nodded. He put his hand on his shoulder and spoke quietly. "Listen, not a word about this to anyone, you hear? If anyone asks, you weren't there. Last thing I need is for everyone to think I was getting tangled up with those boys again."

Mark nodded. "I'll tell you everything later," he said, then he turned back for the lodge.

Felix's eyes lit up. "Wait! Something I forgot to—"

"Hold on a minute, there!"

Mark's hand was on the door handle. He turned his head and realized the sheriff was talking and pointing at him. Mark tried to put on a pleasant smile.

"I recognize you from the last time I was here," Hank said, coming to a stop next to Felix.

"Yeah, that's right," Mark said. "I seem to remember you, too."

"Well I just realized I never got your name," Hank said, offering a smile.

"It's Mark. Mark Winters."

"Hank Driscoll," he said, extending his hand. Mark shook it. After a few firm shakes, he let go, but Hank continued his grip for a moment longer.

"It was nice meeting you, but if you'll excuse me, I've got some things I've got to get done," Mark said, pointing his thumb back at the lodge.

Hank looked at him suspiciously. "Well listen, I've got some questions I intend to ask you, so if you can tell me how you're staying at a vacation resort and you have important things to do, I guess I can let you off the hook."

Mark swallowed. "Shoot."

"I thought you'd see things my way," Hank said. He patted Mark hard on the shoulder. Felix stayed on the sidelines, observing the conversation with an uneasy look on his face.

"You know," Hank started, "it seems to me I was here at this lodge... well, just yesterday. Someone tried to burn the place down. Now someone explodes that house up there in the hills. Nothing like this has ever happened around this neck of the woods before, and it all happens right around the time you show up. Little suspicious, don't you think?"

Mark was dumbstruck. He wanted to say something—anything—to assuage the sheriff's accusations, but he didn't know how he could deny it.

Hank let out a hearty laugh. His face went rosy as his hand clamped tight on Mark's shoulder. "I'm just playin' around."

Mark laughed too, and his smile thinned a little quicker than he intended.

Hank's face turned to stone. "In all seriousness, though, why are you here?"

"What do you mean?" Mark asked.

"Well, I mean that it's rainy season. The only customers Felix sees in the rainy season are diehards. Not only that, but you decided to stay at the lodge during the biggest storm Clemington's seen in decades? Which, by my watch, is supposed to be here any minute today." Hank looked at the clouds forming on the edge of the sky. "I'm surprised we aren't blowing away already." He turned back to Mark. "And I know you're probably a real out-of-towner—no offence—but it seems like you might have a different reason for being here than the fishing."

Mark stayed quiet. He stared at Hank, wondering what he should tell him. He obviously couldn't tell him the truth. It was such a long and extravagant story. Not a lick of it he would believe.

Felix stepped in. "You're right; he didn't come here for the fishing. Mark's here to clear his head. He's going through a bit of a tragedy right now and he needed some place where he could be alone."

Hank looked from Felix to Mark. "I'm real sorry to hear that. You have my condolences.

"So how about that explosion, then?" Hank asked, changing the subject. "Know anything about that?"

Mark shook his head. "No, I didn't find out about it until this morning; I was sleeping when it happened."

"You slept through an explosion?" Hank said in a tone that underscored how ridiculous his statement was. "The entire *town* heard that explosion, and you were just down the hill from it."

Mark shrugged. "Heavy sleeper, I guess." After a few seconds, he added: "I'd been through a lot the night before and I was pretty much out of it the whole night."

"Speaking of that, where were you last night?"

"Here in the lodge."

"The whole night?"

Mark felt like he was walking into a trap. "Yes," he said cautiously, and he saw Felix wince.

"That's funny," Hank said, "because Felix gave our department a call last night and said that you were missing. Said he looked all over the grounds out here and couldn't find you. He was afraid that you'd come back all crazy like Pete did, if I recall correctly."

Shit, Mark thought. That must have been what Felix was about to warn him of when Hank arrived.

He looked down at his feet like a dog who just did something wrong and sighed. "Felix said that I'm going through a tragedy. Well, the truth is... my family was murdered a couple days ago. It's been such a crazy experience that I often don't know what to do with myself. I came to this lodge because I was here with my dad and my brother once when I was young, and it reminded me of an easier time. Last night, I sort of fell into a bit of a panic attack. With all this crazy stuff happening, and with Pete coming in like he did last night, I just had to leave and get some fresh air."

"Where'd you go?" Hank asked. "Bit of a goose egg on your forehead, there."

"Hit my head on a tree in the dark," Mark answered, rubbing the spot. "Bit of a klutz, I guess. I ended up taking a trek into the woods. Not the smartest thing to do in the dead of night, I know, but I just needed to clear my head. I ended up getting lost, and it wasn't until maybe an hour later that I found my way back to the lodge. I was so embarrassed by the whole thing that I was reluctant to tell the truth."

"So you saw the explosion?" Hank asked.

"Um... yeah."

"Well? Did you see anything other than 'Um, yeah'? A perpetrator, maybe?"

"No, just a big ball of fire. I was taking a walk on the other side of the lake when it happened," Mark lied.

"And you didn't think to come right to the authorities?" Hank said sternly.

"Lot on my mind, like I said," Mark offered. "I was exhausted when I got back to the lodge. I went straight to bed and didn't wake up until now."

Hank sized him up and down, then he finally nodded. "Well don't let me keep you from your important business. That's all the questions I have."

"Thanks," Mark said, relieved that the inquisition was over.

"Felix, I'll talk to you in a little bit," Hank said.

Felix nodded.

Hank started to turn when he stopped suddenly. His eyes were fixated on Mark's leg. "What happened there?"

Mark looked down. A small spot of blood stained the front of his pant leg. He and Felix exchanged a worried look. "I cut myself yesterday morning in a little fishing mishap," he said. "The stitches must have ripped."

"I thought you weren't here for the fishing," Hank said, his face returning to that deadly serious look. A long, very uncomfortable silence hung in the air. Mark stared at Hank's intense eyes, having no response to offer him.

A tall man dressed in a high-ranking firefighter's uniform approached Hank from behind and tapped on his shoulder. His white hair was trimmed short and he had a long, gaunt face that gave the impression he wasn't a fan of anything other than business.

Hank turned around. "Bernie, how ya doin'? What's the word?"

"That's what I came to talk to you about," Bernie said. He spoke with a careful slowness. "Do you mind if we talk in private?"

"Not at all," Hank said, motioning up the path.

Bernie put a hand on Hank's shoulder and led him out of earshot.

Mark and Felix stood silently, watching the two of them talk. Bernie mouthed something and Hank immediately turned his head and looked at Felix. He nodded then headed off toward the wreckage up the hill.

Bernie came back down the path to Mark and Felix.

"Mark, this is the fire chief, Bernie," Felix said. "Bernie, this is Mark. He's a guest here."

"You're staying here right before the storm?" Bernie asked.

Mark chuckled. "Yeah, I've heard."

"Listen, Felix, my men were poring over the wreckage up there and they found something you might be interested in. Well, they found *a lot* of what you might be interested in."

"What?" Felix asked.

"They found human remains."

"Of the brothers?"

"I'm not talking about them. I'm talking about long-dried human bones. Some of them were tiny fragments, but there are a lot of bigger pieces that are still intact. They're scattered all over the place, and there's a lot of them. Probably enough to fill an entire basement. You were right; it looks like these boys were the killers you made them out to be the entire time. You should be proud of yourself."

Felix stared off at the wreckage. His face held a very tense look, like he was trying to hold back tears.

"I just thought you should know," Bernie said.

"What about the brothers?" Felix asked.

"We've found three charred bodies in the debris. The blast did quite a number on them. One was just a torso; another one was missing his head. Seeing as how we don't have dental records of the brothers, there's nothing to match. But I don't think it's much of a stretch to assume that they're your boys. And I think it's safe to say they won't be killing anyone ever again."

Bernie shook Felix's hand and nodded at Mark, then he set off back toward the wreckage.

Felix couldn't hold back any longer. Tears streamed down his face. His countenance was one of utter triumph and happiness. He practically beamed at Mark.

But Mark looked at him cautiously. "Felix..."

"What?"

"He said they found three bodies."

"I know," Felix said, smiling.

"When they kidnapped me last night, there was another person alive in the house."

"*What?*" Felix said.

Mark nodded. "Cleaver killed him, but... that should be *four* bodies they found."

Felix's eyes went wide. "One of them's still out there."

Mark nodded.

"Maybe they didn't find his body yet," Felix reasoned.

Mark sighed. "Let's hope so."

Felix looked bewildered, like he didn't know what to think. "I think I'll go... take a look," he said. His eyes flitted back and forth in his head, like his brain was processing a lot of information all at once. And without another word he turned and left up the hill.

Mark watched him go and he recognized another face as it bobbed past Felix down the hill.

Hector spotted Mark and waved, hurrying over to him. "Mark, there you are!" he said. "Can you believe this mess?"

"I'm just glad those brothers are gone," Mark said.

"Amen to that," Hector said, taking his hat off and rumpling his hair. "They've always given me the creeps. I've always been glad to live on the opposite side of the cove from them. It gave me an if-ever-so-slight peace of mind." He lost himself in reverie for a moment then remembered why he came over to Mark in the first place.

"I forgot to mention," he said. "I dug out more of Nathaniel's journals this morning. These ones I had stashed away in a place I completely forgot about. Mark... I think I found something."

Mark couldn't help but get excited, even though he had no idea what Hector was talking about. "What?"

"I'm not entirely sure, and I want to cross-check some other sources from Nathaniel just to be certain. I'm heading into town for a little while today, but I'll stop by the lodge later this evening with the details, one way or another."

"Hector, what is it?"

"There may be a way to save your brother."

— CHAPTER TWENTY —

The Storm Arrives

At about two-thirty in the afternoon, the storm arrived. Just like everyone predicted, it was the biggest storm Clemington had seen in over four decades. A nasty hurricane on the east coast got the worst of it and sent the remainder inland. Because Clemington was in the northwest corner of South Carolina, it was usually protected from storms and hurricanes that people on the east coast were ravaged by. Because of this, the small population of Clemington generally wasn't prepared for bad storms, but with all the hype of this one, everyone came prepared. That included Felix.

By mid-afternoon, the storm had already started bending trees nearly in half as harsh rain battered anything in its path, and it was just warming up. After the firefighters and police finished looking over the wreckage, taking from it what evidence they felt most imperative to have and trying their best to cover the rest with tightly-fastened tarps, they left just after noon.

Soon after, Mark helped Felix go around the lodge and make sure everything was tied down. The first thing they did was round up the boats sitting out in the water and secured them in the boathouse. After that, they spent most of their time covering all the windows of the lodge with wooden boards. By the time they finished, the wind had become very fierce and they could barely stand outside without being blown away.

Mark told Felix everything about his night in the brothers' house. He spared no detail from seeing Cleaver standing outside the lounge window through to his escape. As he told the story, Felix seemed happy and at peace with what happened to the brothers, but he also had a slight vibe that Mark interpreted as disappointment. Disappointment at not being the one to take down the brothers himself, he figured. After Felix had spent most of his life crusading after this cause, Mark understood that this whole situation was complicated for him, to say the least.

They mostly sat at the bar for the rest of the day. Mark was very eager for Hector to show up and hoped that he made it through the storm okay. When evening hit, Felix made his way to the kitchen and cooked him and Mark some supper. They ate in silence, and after finishing, they returned to waiting at the bar. Occasionally, each of them would glance up at the clock on the wall and take note of how slowly time seemed to be moving. Felix seemed more on edge than usual—understandably. He had the shotgun hidden behind the bar, but Mark knew what he was looking at every time his eyes wandered in that direction.

Eventually, when Felix was running dangerously low on toothpicks from nervously chewing on them, he went behind the bar and poured some drinks. Mark decided it was okay to indulge a little bit, but he restrained himself from overdoing it, remembering that he nearly drowned the last time. Mark proposed a toast to Jerry and Pete, and said a solemn word in Pete's memory. Felix gave a strained smile and quietly tended to his drink.

At nine-thirty, the interior of the lodge was completely dark, save for the lights shining overhead in the lounge, the light coming in through the thin gaps in the boarded windows faded now. It gave off a creepy vibe, like something sinister was waiting for them just outside of their lonely and isolated light.

Mark had brought out Nathaniel's secret ledger that he stored in his room and leafed through parts of it. Still offering no apparent answers, he left it on the bar, and a little while after that Felix picked it up and started to peruse it out of sheer boredom. When his throat started to get a little dry, he took the book with him behind the bar and continued skimming through it as he poured himself a drink.

At just past ten o'clock, the lounge doors flew open. At first, Mark and Felix thought the severe wind from the storm had done it and were surprised when they saw a rather spooked-looking Hector standing sopping wet in the doorway. He came in and wrenched the doors shut behind him. He stood with his mouth agape, like he'd just seen something he couldn't believe. After a moment, he looked down and noticed what a mess he'd made on the floor. He glanced at Felix in apology and Felix waved him away. He took off his large rain poncho and left it crumpled on the floor by the doors, then nervously wrung his hands together as he looked back and forth from Felix to Mark, as if waiting for an acknowledgement.

Felix sighed. "It's okay, Hector. Come have a seat. Don't worry about the floors."

Hector gave an absent-minded nod and a weak "Thanks", then he carefully made his way to the stool next to Mark, his boots squeaking along the way.

Mark turned in his seat, eager to know what he was investigating. "So, did you find what you were looking for?"

Hector seemed more interested in his hat as he took it off, inspected it for a moment, then shook it violently over the floor. He ran a hand through his wiry white hair and slicked it back, wringing water from it. He took another look at his hat then replaced it on his head.

"Hector?" Mark said.

"Hmm? Oh! Yes... sorry." Hector fidgeted in his seat and leaned on the bar. "Like I told you earlier, I found some more of Nathaniel's journals... ones I haven't read for a long time. You see, I was thinking about your brother and how he's been trying to get you to go to that cabin on the island. And there was something always bugging me... something I seem to remember reading in one of Nathaniel's journals a long time ago. And when I found these particular journals, I found what I was looking for."

"A way to help my brother," Mark said impatiently.

"That's right. Now, these are some of Nathaniel's later journals. They were written by him after he'd been researching the strange presence on the island for quite a long time. There are no dates written on any of the entries, but judging from their contents, it seems like he wrote them after the police raided the lodge and he seemingly disappeared. In these journals, he mentions underground catacombs that he built."

"He mentioned his idea to build that before," Mark chimed in.

"Right," Hector said. "And he actually did it. He said the entrance is a particular grave in an old cemetery, but he didn't say where the graveyard is." Hector slumped on the bar and rested his chin on his hands. "That's the only part I can't figure out."

Mark's eyes lit up. "I know where."

"You do?"

"Yeah, he mentioned where he was going to do it in one of the journals you gave me. But the journals burned up in the fire."

"Do you remember what it said?" Hector pressed, hopeful.

Mark searched the corners of his mind. "'*One mile due west of the lake.*' That's what he said."

"Hmm... that might be enough to find it," Hector said. He looked at Mark very carefully. "Now, I have to warn you... Nathaniel mentioned what he used these catacombs for. And some of the things..." He trailed off.

"What?" Mark said. "Some of the things what?"

"They're a little out there," Hector said with some trepidation.

"What, like torture?"

"Well, yes, but... there's more."

"Well, *what is it?*" Mark asked pointedly.

"I just want you to prepare yourself. You see, there are things that Nathaniel has alleged that he's done down there that may not make sense. Some things that seem like they break the very laws of biology. Things that seem at place only in nightmares."

Mark was taken aback. "Like what?"

"I don't know," Hector admitted. "He was vague on the details. I just want you to prepare yourself for anything."

"Noted," Mark said, his eyes trailing off. "What about Jamie? How do I help him?"

"Well," Hector started, "Nathaniel also mentioned being able to bring someone back to life."

A rush of excitement and trepidation rose up in Mark. "Back... to *life?* Did he say how?"

"Not in his journals. But he constantly made mention of a book of rituals that he kept with him. Apparently he did many experiments where he would bring a victim that he'd killed back to life just so he could experiment on them some more. It's probably the worst agony you could imagine. He said in one passage that all the secrets of how to bring someone back from the dead were detailed in this ritual book of his."

"And I'm guessing the book is in the catacombs," Mark said.

"Nathaniel always talked about keeping the book close to him, so originally it wasn't. But in his last journal, he talked about laying himself to rest in a special tomb he built for himself down in his catacombs. It seems old age got the better of him and he had accomplished just about everything he'd wanted in his life. He said that he would bury himself with that book, so that's where it must be."

"Do you really think this could save my brother?" Mark asked. "I want to say this sounds too ridiculous, but I've seen plenty of that since coming here. Do you... do you think my brother could have a normal life again?"

"I can't say for sure, but it seems likely," Hector said. "Nathaniel was very powerful."

Mark thought on this. "But if Nathaniel figured out how to bring someone back to life, why did he die? Couldn't he just bring himself back?"

Hector shrugged. "Your guess is as good as mine. Like I said, maybe he was content with what he accomplished and was genuinely ready for death. And maybe that's why the brothers seemed to have taken such an interest in him lately. Maybe they discovered this miraculous feat and wanted to use it to resurrect him. Not that it matters anymore, I suppose."

"There's still one of them out there," Mark said.

Hector looked confused. "What do you mean?"

"The fire chief said they only found three bodies in the wreckage. One of them was a victim that I saw in the house before I blew it up."

"That was *you?*" Hector said in disbelief.

Mark nodded.

"So... which one of them is still alive?"

"I don't know," Mark said. "I don't know for sure if any of them survived. Maybe they just didn't find the body yet. I mean, they didn't really have a lot of time before the storm came in. But it's possible that one of them is still out there, planning to resurrect Nathaniel."

"You've got to find that book," Hector said with a sudden certainty.

"I know," Mark said. "I'll do it—I *have* to. It's because of me that my entire family is dead, and if I can save my brother... God, I'll give anything." He looked over at Felix and realized that he hadn't said a single word since Hector came in. "Felix, will you help me?"

Felix stared down at his empty tumbler for a long moment. "No."

Mark was shocked. His mouth hung open, not knowing how to react.

"I didn't say anything all day," Felix said, "but I was mulling it over in my head. And I think it's time that you left."

"*What?*" Mark cried. "Why?"

"I like you, Mark, I really do. But ever since you've come here, I've had nothing but trouble. Pete is *dead*, for

God's sake. And now you're talking about all this silly horseshit about tomb raiding? I won't ask you to go now, because of the storm."

"But... but... my *brother!*" Mark sputtered.

"You shouldn't be messing around with any of this shit," Felix said. "You've got your health... be thankful for that. Don't go throwing it away on something as crazy as this."

"Felix, you don't understand. I can *save* him."

"You *think* you can save him," Felix said. "Have you listened to yourself with all this nonsense? That's all it is: nonsense. Listen, man, count the blessings you have left and walk away. That's what I would do."

"That's what you would do?" Mark snapped. "Just let it go and walk away? Is that why your wife walked out on you and you haven't seen your daughter in thirty years?"

As soon as he said it, a painful silence came over the room and he wished he could take the words back.

"Felix, I'm sorry," he started, "but my brother needs me. Every day he's been calling out to me for help. I'm the one who did this to him and I'm the only one who can save him. I *need* to do this."

He waited, half-expecting Felix to get angry, but instead he was calm.

"Tomorrow when the storm eases up a bit, I want you gone," Felix said.

"Fine," Mark said. "But until then, I'm going to that tomb." He turned to Hector. "What about you?"

Hector suddenly became very sheepish. He took off his straw hat and bunched it up in his hands. "I, uh... I'm afraid I'm, well... *terrified* of the dark. I don't think I'd be much help to you."

Mark put his head down on the bar. Dizzying images and thoughts swirled in his head. "Whatever. Just tell me how I get into this damn place."

Hector straightened out his hat and put it back on his head. He eyed Mark nervously as he spoke, almost expecting Mark to lash out at him. "Remember that strange symbol you showed me that you said was carved into your door? He developed that symbol as his brand, so to speak—the symbol of the Black Warden. That same symbol is etched into a specific grave in the cemetery. It's supposed to mark the entrance to his catacombs."

"So which grave is it?"

"I don't know. You'll have to find it by that symbol."

A thought suddenly occurred to Mark. "You said the book is buried in the tomb with Nathaniel. If one of the brothers might be out there trying to resurrect him, what should I do with his body if it's right there with the book?"

Hector nodded, realizing that he'd never thought of that before. "You should stop that from happening, any way you can. It's up to your discretion to decide how to do that."

"Okay. I'll figure something out."

Hector stood up and put on his rain poncho. "Mark, there's one more thing."

"What is it?"

"I know now might not be the best time to mention it, but Nathaniel said that the catacombs are guarded by the 'Sentinel'."

Mark's jaw hung open. "The *what?*"

"I wish I knew," Hector said. "Just... be careful."

And with that, he left into the howling storm.

Mark stood rooted in place, dumbfounded at what he'd just heard. He finally turned and looked at Felix who was still staring at the empty tumbler in front of him. He opened his mouth to say something, but decided against it. He walked to the doors and paused in front of them. After a long moment, he pulled them open and went out into the stormy night.

The doors slammed shut, echoing throughout the empty lodge.

Felix sat in silence. He twisted the tumbler around in his fingers for a while, then he threw it across the room. It collided with the wall next to the charred library and shattered to pieces. After the sounds of twinkling glass falling to the floor stopped he was once again left with the grating sound of the wind and rain. He let out a long breath.

He glanced over the bar top and spied Nathaniel's black ledger he'd left behind it. He grabbed it and continued reading where he left off. He finished the page and flipped to the next one. Once he got halfway down the new page, his eyes stopped on something.

"Son of a bitch," he muttered. He got to his feet and rushed over to the lounge doors. He pulled them open and stepped outside. Shielding his eyes from the pouring rain, he peered into the distance in the direction Mark went.

But he was already gone.

— CHAPTER TWENTY-ONE —

Grave Robbing

He made it about halfway to the graveyard before he strongly considered turning back. The storm was far fiercer than he had anticipated, the trees in the woods not giving him much in the way of cover. His clothes were soaked and stuck to his skin, and his shoes were like sopping puddles themselves.

The wind whipped huge drops of water in his face so hard that it felt like he was being pelted by stones. Still, he pressed on.

The storm clouds were so thick and heavy that it was almost pitch-black outside. He caught faint glimpses of something through the woods here and there, his heart rising in anticipation each time, only to be dashed when it turned out to be a strange shadow or thin clearing in the woods.

But then he saw something up ahead. He shielded his eyes and squinted to be sure, but there was a break in the woods ahead, larger than he'd seen before. The barren forest floor turned into thick, overgrown grass. And in the dim light, row upon row of tall headstones were fixed in the ground.

Mark smiled and the rain pelted him in the teeth. His body was already exhausted, having fought through the fierce winds to get here, but he finally made it and soon he would have shelter from the bitter storm.

He gulped. The chill of the catacombs, wherever they were, called to him and stymied his joy. Cemeteries had always made him feel uncomfortable, but knowing what was underneath it was especially sobering.

He broke into the clearing and his feet sank into the marshy grass. The moonlight was very dim, but it offered just enough light to read the tombstones if he was close enough. He crouched by the closest one and shielded his eyes from the torrential rain.

Freddie Rose – 1831-1878

Mark touched the gravestone, patting his hands all around it and then trying to wiggle it in the ground. He stood on the plot before the stone, feeling morbid, and stamped his feet down on the ground, splashing water about.

He knew the entrance was in a particular grave somewhere in this cemetery, but he had no idea which one. He didn't know exactly where he had wandered from the lodge, but he was pretty sure he had walked in a relatively straight line, and though it felt a lot longer due to the storm, it must have been about a mile out; this had to be the place.

His eyes stretched across the endless rows of plots and headstones and he gulped. His body shivered from the endless volley of cold, stinging rain. He went to the next headstone and inspected it, but found nothing of interest. Mark's mind raced, trying to determine how any of these plots or stones could house some kind of entrance.

After checking a few stones in the first row, he moved to the next one, and then the one after that, and then broke into a jog through the long-forgotten graveyard, casting short glances left and right as he went. The thought that this was all some cruel joke being played on him welled up in his mind, but he pressed it back down.

When he was about to give up hope, he skirted around some very tall and wild bushes crowding into the graveyard and saw something behind it.

A small mausoleum sat in the back corner of the graveyard. It was the only thing that stood out from the rest of the graves, and the only thing that could sensibly house a hidden entrance.

Mark crouched against it and shielded himself from the storm. He cupped his hands around his eyes so he could see better and looked the small structure up and down. It was no bigger than eight by eight feet with a stone door sealing it. But there was no handle or any indication of how to open it. Mark pushed on the door and tried to squeeze his fingernails into the cracks, to no avail.

"Come on," he muttered miserably.

He searched the stone bricks that made up the mausoleum for any kind of clue or indication of how to gain entrance. Turning the corner to the side of it, he saw something near the roof: a tiny etching was made into one of the bricks, so small that it was almost imperceptible. But it looked familiar to him, and as he leaned in and got a closer look, he recognized it right away: the same symbol that Hunter carved into his door in the lodge; the symbol of the Black Warden.

He raised his hand timidly, afraid that it would be too good to be true, then he gently pressed his fingers against the brick. It slid an inch inward.

The ground shook and the door scraped against the masonry.

Mark returned to the front, excitement making his heart pound. The stone door lowered into the ground until it revealed a blackened tomb beyond. He expected to see a casket lying inside, but the dim light shining just in the entrance of the doorway showed nothing but an empty floor. Mark held out his hands and crept inside. He reached into his wallet and took out the matchbook, frowning at the sogginess of the paper. But the matches inside were dry. He plucked one out of the book and dragged it along the striker.

The light of the flame illuminated what appeared at first to be an empty room. But the floor was strange, visibly not attached to the wall on any side. And there was a lever fixed to the stone in front of him. He was standing in an elevator.

A lantern hung on a hook in the wall next to it, and he grabbed it and lit it with his match before it went out. To his surprise, there was still kerosene inside. He gave one last look at the howling storm outside. He was soaking wet and felt a cold chill come up through the cracks in the floor. As he glanced at the lever, a dizzying, maddening feeling came over him at what he was doing. It was crazy, but he had come too far to turn back. All he had to do was get the book and get out.

The Sentinel, a small voice whispered in his head.

He ignored it. He reached for the lever and felt the cold steel under his hand. Mark's breath caught in his throat. His mind raced. He stared at the lever like it was the most terrible thing he had ever seen. And then, with a deep breath, he pulled it down.

The steel wrenched against the frame and unseen gears beneath him ground into motion. The floor hitched and sank an inch, almost causing him to lose his footing. Then the gears turned smoothly and the floor descended down the long shaft. The air became increasingly colder and he felt a weak gust climb up the darkness and through the cracks between the elevator and the walls.

Mark stared up and saw the tiny rectangle of light and the sound of the storm steadily fade away. The ride seemed to take forever, and for a moment he thought he was descending straight to Hell.

Finally, the elevator stopped with a jerk and Mark stumbled into the wall. He turned and saw a long, dark corridor stretch in front of him. The walls looked like they had been crudely carved out of subterranean stone, with thick dust and cobwebs covering them.

"*Get the book and get out,*" Mark whispered to himself. "*Get the book and get out.*" His voice echoed hideously along the corridor. He heard it fade into the distance and then rebound, coming back to him in a mockery of the original. He felt a deep chill that had nothing to do with the cold, and he pressed into the blackness ahead.

He held the lantern in front of him. The ceiling wasn't much higher than his head and he constantly felt cobwebs stroking his face as he broke their seal and plunged himself headlong into the unknown. The thick layer of ashy dust on the stone floor caked to the bottoms of his wet shoes. Braziers adorned the walls. They looked so old and strewn with cobwebs that Mark wondered if they would even light anymore. He ignored them and continued on.

Mark plucked a strand of webbing out of his eyes as a spider scurried down his shoulder. The lantern cleared the darkness away ahead and he came to a wall as the path branched left and right. He stared in each direction, seeing nothing but the same ancient and decrepit corridors as before. A brazier was affixed to the wall in front of him. If he was entering a maze, it would be a good idea to light his path so he could find his way back.

He took another match out of the soggy matchbook and ignited it. Clearing the cobwebs away with his free hand, he held the flame to the dusty charcoals and was surprised to see them ignite. The flames danced and flicked, casting strange movement across the stone walls. It cast a farther light than the lantern and made Mark feel a bit of warmth. But the coldness of the dark chasm seeped out and wrapped its icy fingers around him, daring him to come further.

After some consideration, Mark took the path on the right. Whenever he came to a fork, he would light a nearby brazier to mark his passing. The corridors twisted and turned and bent and curved. He tried to keep an active map of it in his mind, but he was quickly losing track of it. He prayed that he would find Nathaniel's tomb soon so he could snatch the book and be on his way, following the light back to the elevator and never having to lay eyes on such an accursed place again.

Mark rounded the corner and stepped on something. It was brittle and broke under his foot. He lifted his leg and lowered the lantern. The crumpled top half of a human skull peered up at him. He recoiled and pulled his leg away out of fear. He kicked his shoe on the wall, loosening the bone fragments from his sole. He cast the lantern in a wide arc in front of him. More bones were strewn on the ground here or there.

Mark's teeth chattered. He quickened his pace, trying to put the remains out of his mind. He carved his way through the darkness, intense fear clutching at his heart now.

He thought about Nathaniel's body that he would inevitably find with the ritual book. Methods of disposal came to mind and he mulled over each one carefully.

The corridor connected to a large room with tall stone slabs that looked like altars. Dark-red stains were tattooed into the stones. The room was otherwise empty, but there was a large hole in the floor in the center of the room. An intense smell of decay and other oddities rose up from the hole and Mark had to pinch his nose to keep from throwing up.

The kerosene in the lantern was thinning, and he knew he would have to hurry. He took another exit out of the room and came to a fork in the path, this one offering three directions. He went straight. The bones lining the corridors became more frequent. He was mindful of where he stepped. He listened to the sound of his own footsteps marching down the lonely path, followed by nothing but silence.

Clop, clop, clop.

He took a left and felt a cold breeze run over his skin from some unseen vent in the stone. His wet body shivered. He walked on.

Clop, clop, clop.

Slap, slap, slap.

Mark stopped. There was no sound except for his heartbeat and the flickering of some distant brazier's fire. He kept walking.

Clop, clop, clop.

Slap, slap, slap.

He stopped again. Silence. The other sound had been layered behind his footsteps, making it hard to discern what it was. It reminded him of someone's bare feet slapping against bathroom tile.

Clop... clop, clop.

Slap slap slap slap slap!

Mark broke into a run. The lantern swung wildly from his hand as he hurtled down the dark corridor ahead of him. A fuzzy din settled behind his ears, blocking out everything else around him. His breathing became short and labored. He took different branches in the path, running and running until finally, having gone far enough, he screeched to a stop and turned around. He held the lantern up as his heart pounded.

Whatever had been following him seemed to have stopped. The catacombs were once again silent. Catching his breath and composing himself, Mark turned around.

He was in a large room. The ceiling stretched too high into the shadows for him to see it. The walls on either side of him were just barely in the fringes of the lantern's light, and what awaited him ahead was shrouded in darkness and mystery. He crept forward, letting the light inch over the terrain. At first he thought the room was empty, but soon he came upon a platform about two feet high sitting at the back of the room. A doorway—another entrance into the room, or perhaps an exit—sat to the left. Then the lantern's light climbed up the platform until it illuminated a large stone sarcophagus atop it. A large curtain hung on the wall behind the sarcophagus. It was red with thick gold embroidery stitched into it, forming a symbol: the Black Warden's symbol.

Mark gasped. This was it. This was Nathaniel's resting place and what he had come for. He glanced at the doorway to the left but could see only darkness. He gazed behind him to see if something was lurking. All he had to do was get the book, if nothing else, and go back the way he came, following the lights he had lit along the twisting corridors.

He stared at the sarcophagus. He thought of turning back, but he couldn't. Setting the lantern down on the platform, he stepped onto it and gently rested his hands on the stone lid of the sarcophagus. It was colder than he thought it would be. His clothes had started to dry over his long trek through the catacombs, but now a hot sweat broke out on his skin.

For Jamie, Mark thought. *It's all for Jamie.*

He pushed on the edge of the lid. It was incredibly heavy and he had to hunker down and use all the strength he had to move it. It began to slide inch by inch, filling the large room with an incredibly loud and irritating grating noise. He pushed and pushed, the veins in his neck bulging. When he moved it halfway, it teetered on the edge, then it fell behind the sarcophagus and cracked apart, sending a tremor through the room.

Exhausted, Mark picked up the lantern and backed off. He beheld the open sarcophagus from the floor below, too frightened to see what was inside. When he worked up the courage, he stepped onto the platform and held the light over the huge stone coffin.

Inside, there was no body. There was no ritual book. It was completely empty except for a yellowed piece of parchment.

"*What?*" Mark demanded to the empty room. He felt sick to his stomach. With a shaking hand, he bent and picked the scrap of parchment up, holding it to the light. As he read it, his eyes widened and he nearly fainted.

The Black Warden's return is close at hand

— CHAPTER TWENTY-TWO —

THE SENTINEL

That was all the note said. Mark stood there dumbfounded for a long time. He turned the note over in his hand, but there was nothing else written on it. Refusing to believe what he found, he leaned over the sarcophagus and inspected every inch of the interior for something that he must have missed. But it was clearly empty.

Someone had been here before him. That was it. He was too late, too late to stop what was going to happen, and now he was stuck underground, his chances of returning to the surface fading away quicker than his hope. But he had to escape; if someone was going to resurrect Nathaniel soon, he had to warn Felix. He had to warn Hector, warn *everybody*.

Mark turned back for the door he came through.

The room began to rumble. The lantern swayed in his hand. A stone door rose up from the ground and sealed the corridor off. Mark ran up to it, shoving on it, wedging his fingers in the cracks and pulling, but it didn't budge. He spun around quickly and looked at the only other exit from the room. It was still open, but he didn't take any chances. He sprinted over to it and entered a corridor similar to all of the others he had traversed through. He stood just inside of it and held the lantern in front of him.

The kerosene was getting low. He wouldn't have much time.

Slap, slap, slap.

Mark's heart jumped. Somewhere in the distance the bloodcurdling sound played. It was so soft and innocent, but Mark couldn't shake his fear of it.

The Sentinel, his mind said as if it was wide-eyed and pointing into the darkness. He tried to ignore it, but this time he couldn't. The good news was that if he heard the same sounds here, that meant all of these tunnels were connected and if he chose his paths correctly, he would be able to find his way back to the elevator. The bad news was that something might be waiting for him.

He started down the corridor. The air was stuffy. Warmer than before. An unnerving silence held over the catacombs long enough to make his skin crawl. He passed through a large room with short but deep slots in the wall, stacked up in unending rows and columns. Skeletons were nestled in most of them, each slot big enough for just one body. Some of the skulls had come to rest facing outward, now staring at Mark as he passed through, on their long road to disintegration. The smell was horrible and reminded him of the brothers' basement. He wanted to vomit, but he kept it together. He quickened his pace.

He took different forks in the path, trying to cobble together the map that he had first created when he came down here. It was a complete mess, but he prayed he was heading in the right direction. He rounded a corner and followed the corridor as it continued into the blackness ahead. He came upon a small boulder blocking half of the narrow pathway. Its appearance was strange to him at first, its surface seeming more like leather than stone. Mark squeezed to the left side of the tunnel, preparing to move past it, when suddenly it stood up.

Mark cried out in fear and stumbled backward. He pulled the lantern with him, taking the frightening thing in the corridor out of range of the light. Now it was just a black silhouette ahead, barely visible. It breathed softly. Then it started to run.

Mark turned around and ran for his life. Tears wet his face as it scrunched up in pleas of mercy to any god that would listen. He didn't dare look over his shoulder.

Slap slap slap slap. The heavy footfalls came for him and Mark took a right at the fork ahead. He couldn't remember if he had come from this way or the other, but now he was acting only on instinct. This thing chasing him had incredible quickness, and he heard the footfalls quickly gain on him.

The creature moaned—an awful, aching sound—filling the entire corridor like a blaring siren. It made Mark's whole body convulse in disgust.

As Mark rounded the corner of another branching corridor, his foot slipped on a bone on the floor. His legs slipped out from under him and he crashed to the ground. The thick layer of dust was shoved up into the air and wafted, making him cough.

The Sentinel moaned right behind him.

As Mark tried to get up, he twisted around and held the lantern over his head, both to illuminate and to block the coming attack, knowing the creature was upon him. The Sentinel came into view of the lantern's light and Mark almost fainted from the sight of it.

It was entirely human, but yet it was nothing of the sort. It had the same apparent anatomy and shape of a human, but each limb, each individual piece of the creature, was cobbled together from a different body, like Dr. Frankenstein's monster. The skin on its bald head was leathery and loose-fitting. Its face looked like the skin had been stitched onto a skull that didn't match. Its eyes were white, the irises and pupils faded to almost nothing. The skeleton seemed to be cobbled together at slightly different angles than normal, perhaps explaining the incredible speed. But it was so close to the lantern now that its chest and head blocked the light, leaving the rest of its anatomy covered in darkness below.

Mark screamed. Something whipped by in the light and ripped the lantern out of his hand. The lantern smashed into the wall and the flame inside extinguished, leaving Mark in darkness. He spun around and tried to clamber up to his feet, but something caught his ankle. He hit the floor hard and his chin knocked onto the dusty stone. He was dragged backward in the darkness and he dug his fingernails into the stone to try to stop it from happening. The flesh gripping his ankle felt dry and sandy on his skin, and yet soft and rubbery at the same time. Mark kicked at the monstrosity with his free leg, and disgusting, squishing sounds were made with each blow that connected. But they seemed to do nothing to deter the creature.

Mark bucked off the ground like a flopping fish and brought his heel down on the wrist holding his ankle, breaking the grip and loosening his foot. He shot up to his feet and tore through the darkness, his hands held out in front of him to keep from running into a wall. He couldn't see a thing, but that didn't slow him down at all.

He collided and bounced off the walls of the decrepit catacombs like a pinball, his fingers and hands quickly becoming numb from the hard impacts. He had no idea where he was going now, operating only on a prayer. He ran and ran, blocking everything else out, until he got too tired to run anymore. He stopped. He turned around and shielded himself from another blow.

Nothing came.

He listened and found himself in total silence again. Mark fished into his pocket and pulled out the matchbook. After all the braziers he had lit, he found that he had only one match left. He held it as carefully as if it were gold, then he struck it against the book and the flame grew on the match head. The light was dim, but it was like an oasis to him. He held his hand in front of it to keep it from snuffing out and marched forward, trying to find his way back. His body ached, but he wouldn't let himself stop. He listened for the telltale footfalls of the Sentinel. For now it was quiet.

He didn't recognize any of the paths he was going down, insofar as they looked indiscernible from every other path he had been down. Occasional bones littered the pathways, a spot of blood here or there, but nothing that told him he was going in the right direction. He imagined with an internal horror that he was climbing farther and farther into the pit of the earth and suddenly the fanciful and grotesque image of his arm poking out from under the lid of his own coffin and nailing it shut flashed before his eyes.

There was a path that branched off on the left just up ahead, and he took it. There, far in the distance, was a flickering light.

Mark's heart leapt in joy. The distant flame danced in the old, dusty brazier; Mark had been here before. He quickened his pace. Another corridor branched off at the brazier and he took it. More lights stood in the distance.

He was doing it. He was really going to find a way out of this nightmare. He followed the twisting path, beginning to recognize some of the subtle cues in the walls and stonework, even a particular cobweb here or there. And with one more bend in the path, he spotted the first brazier he'd lit; the elevator was just around the corner.

As he approached the light, intense heat nipped at his fingers. He dropped the used-up match and hissed, putting his thumb and forefinger into his mouth to soothe them. But he didn't need the match anymore. When he entered the fringe of the brazier's light, he stopped.

Approaching it at the same distance on the other side, the Sentinel stopped. Its vague shape was hideous in the fringes of the light.

The final branch in the corridor lay ahead, an equal distance between them.

Mark took off running. So did the creature. With tunnel vision, Mark got to the corner and rounded it first. The elevator was somewhere in the darkness ahead. He hurtled headlong into it, hearing the sickening slaps of the creature's bare feet behind him. Its moan rattled the corridor.

"*Please, no!*" Mark muttered without realizing it. His whole body cringed, waiting for the impact. Then in the next moment, he was bowled off his feet and slammed face-first to the ground. A heavy weight lay on his back and the hideous moan was right in his ear. Putrid breath worked its way into his nostrils. And then he felt jagged teeth sink into his shoulder.

Mark screamed as his flesh was torn away. He writhed in agony, struggling to move from under the weight of the creature. Its soft and leathery fingers playfully worked their way over his flesh like a curious child.

Mark's arms splayed out to the sides, his hands slapping around for anything he could find. A rock the size of his palm that had crumbled out of the wall met his hand. His fingers gripped around it and he shoved his foot off the wall with enough force to twist around beneath the creature. He swung the rock and felt it collide with the monster's skull. A gooey splat was accompanied by what sounded like a clunking coconut, and the creature fell off of him.

Mark got up to his feet and ran for the elevator. Like a bolt of lightning, the Sentinel was already on its feet and chasing him down again. But Mark had a little bit of a head start. He slammed into the wall of the elevator in the darkness and fumbled around for the lever. Finding it, he wrenched it upward. The gears creaked and churned slowly, but they moved nonetheless.

The Sentinel released its unbearable moan, filling up the corridor like a noxious cloud.

The elevator began to move beneath Mark and he felt himself ascend.

SLAP SLAP SLAP SLAP!

Something slammed into the side of the platform and the floor shook beneath Mark. The elevator still ascended, but it was slowed down by the weight of the creature hanging off of it, trying to pull itself up. Mark couldn't see any of this in the darkness, and he pressed himself against the back of the shaft, staring up and searching for that distant light from the surface.

The creature's moan turned into more of a scream and then there was the sound of flesh ripping. The weight came off the elevator and it steadily chugged up toward the surface. Mark listened to the creature's cries the whole ride up.

When the sound of the howling storm outside drowned them out and the dim light of the distant and muted moon filled the elevator as it came to a stop at the surface, Mark looked down and saw three fingers, each one a different size and slightly different shape, all sheared off at the base.

Mark galloped over them like they would come back to life and the wind nearly took him off his feet as soon as he landed on the grass. The rain battered down into his shoulder wound, causing him unbearable pain. Mark shielded it with his hand and gazed at it in the faint light now. It was left a bloody mess, a gaping hole where flesh was supposed to be. He felt nauseous, but he knew he had to get back to the lodge.

He stumbled through the storm. He didn't know how he made it, but he slowly and surely did. When the lodge finally came into view, he tumbled down most of the rest of the hill, the strength in his legs giving out completely now. He crawled the rest of the way through the bitter winds and rain. On the gravel pathway at the back of the lodge, he found the strength to get up to his feet and he shoved himself through the doors.

"FELIX!" he bellowed.

The lights were on in the lounge, but he didn't see anyone around. He expected Felix to come around a corner any moment, but he never did. In fact, the only sounds were from the storm outside.

The doors closed behind him on their own and were accompanied by a strange clasping sound he hadn't heard before.

"Felix?"

Mark turned and noticed heavy black felt covering the windows, keeping out any possible light that might creep through them. He tried to pull open the doors, but they were locked, and not from the inside. He turned around and faced the lounge, his eyes widening.

Then the power went out, leaving him in complete darkness.

He felt a lump in his throat and a very cold chill run up his spine, knowing that he was trapped in the darkness with Hunter.

— CHAPTER TWENTY-THREE —

CAT AND MOUSE

The first thing he thought of was Felix. Before he went to the catacombs, Felix was sitting at the bar alone. He would have been easy pickings for Hunter. A tight knot sat at the pit of his stomach, and he could feel twin lines of hot tears rolling down his face through the beads of rainwater.

An unending sea of blackness enveloped the lodge. Hunter was somewhere in it, waiting for him... waiting for him to make a wrong move.

A narrow flash of white light appeared from Felix's bedroom up the stairs.

Mark froze and stared in that direction. Did he see something? It almost looked like a flashlight. He walked toward the stairs.

A barstool caught his foot and he fell to the ground with a loud bang. "*Son of a...*" he whispered, resenting his stupidity. He got to his feet and listened, still keeping his eyes locked on the bedroom. The only sounds in the lodge were the wind and rain.

Did Felix turn that light on? he thought. *Is he still alive?* Maybe he was trying to signal him. Or maybe it was Hunter, luring him into a trap.

Mark again walked toward the stairs, bending and holding his hands out in front of him. He had an awful feeling that what he was doing was a bad idea, but he couldn't stop himself. He crept across the floor as quietly as possible, trying to be gentle on the groaning hardwood.

He reached the staircase and started to climb it. His wide eyes stared at the darkness ahead, visualizing the foreboding doorway to the bedroom with two possibilities beyond it: Felix or Hunter. A sense of unease grew with every step and part of him wanted the stairs to go on forever so he'd never reach the top and find out what was waiting for him.

When he did reach the top, he felt for the doorframe then walked through it.

"*Felix?*" he whispered.

He reached into the darkness, expecting to feel someone's chest. Or feel a cool blade slide into his stomach...

His shins bumped into something soft. He reached down and felt Felix's bed. It was empty.

"*Felix?*" he asked again.

A loud swell of rain echoed from somewhere in the lodge. It sounded like part of the roof had torn open, letting the rain pour through. Just as he turned his head at the noise, piano chords began to ring out from somewhere downstairs. As he stepped through the doorway, he saw that part of the lounge was bathed in faint light. A crescendo of drums reverberated through the room.

The jukebox was on. It dimly lit up the dark lounge around it with its glowing lights as a gong crashed and a quick tinkling of piano keys followed. Mark stood at the top of the stairs, mesmerized, as the familiar sounds of "Love, Reign o'er Me" by The Who played.

But how was the jukebox on if Hunter cut the lodge's power?

He crept down the stairs, looking around for the serial killer. A very troubling feeling gnawed at him at the thought that Hunter could gracefully move through the darkness without being heard. He didn't like the fact that Hunter was guiding him—playing with him, even—but the jukebox provided the only light in the lodge.

He headed to the window beside the jukebox and dug his fingers under the fabric.

Floorboards creaked behind him.

He spun around, his heart giving a wild jump. After scanning the lounge and determining it was empty, he turned his attention back to the window.

Floorboards creaked two feet behind him.

Mark spun around and felt his heart in near-paralytic shock, expecting the knife to plunge into him at any instant. He was even more shocked when he saw there still wasn't anyone there. He pressed his back to the wall and darted his eyes in every direction. Even above the blaring jukebox, he was sure he heard the floorboards groan, but it was impossible for someone to move in and out that quickly. Despite his unnatural talents, it was clear that Hunter was telling him the windows were off-limits in this sick game.

Mark spotted a rack of pool cues attached to the wall behind the pool table. He sidled over to it with his back to the wall, carefully watching the darkness beyond the reach of the jukebox's light. He pulled one of the pool cues out and held it defensively in front of him.

That's when it struck him: the jukebox was on its own breaker. He suddenly remembered Felix telling him this the second night he stayed at the lodge. That meant Hunter didn't cut the power; he only flipped off all the breakers, save for the one governing the jukebox. He had to get the lights back on. But where was the breaker box?

He remembered the rest of that night. There was some faulty wiring connected to that particular breaker and sometimes it shut off. Pete got up to flip it back on when it happened that night. Mark looked toward the hallway leading to the guest rooms on the first floor. That's where Pete went. He disappeared down that hallway and then the jukebox came back on about a minute after that. He remembered hearing Pete go down a flight of stairs.

A basement, he thought. But was turning on the lights a clever idea, or did Hunter turn on the jukebox to lure him down there? Suddenly, Mark thought of a better idea.

He moved across the lounge toward the hallway, gripping the pool cue tightly in both hands. He swiveled his head all around him, as if expecting Hunter to lunge out of the darkness. But he knew exactly where Hunter was, and he had his own trap to set.

He slipped into the darkness of the hallway. The basement must have been somewhere toward the end of it through one of the doors. He walked along the right side of the hall, gently feeling the wall. He glanced over his shoulder at the dim lounge. Hunter was waiting for him to go to the basement, so he would wait for Hunter.

His hands touched the shuttered door of a closet. *Perfect*, he thought. He slid the folding door open and it gave a slight whine, but the bellowing sounds of The Who coming out of the jukebox were more than loud enough to mask any small noises he made. He slipped into the closet and closed the door halfway, leaving enough room for him to jump out when the time was right.

He crouched down and listened, holding the pool cue at the ready. His heart pounded like crazy. At first there was nothing but the noise of the jukebox, but after a few moments he heard floorboards creak somewhere in the lounge. They were coming toward the hallway. Flittering violins played in harmony with them as they made their way closer to the closet. Mark tensed, ready to strike. The footsteps passed the closet and continued down the hallway.

Now! he thought.

The closet door was ripped off its track and tossed away like an unwanted toy. An enormous hand grabbed him around the throat and pulled him out of the closet, slamming him into the wall on the other side of the hallway. He bounced off it and fell to the floor with a loud crash. Mark struggled against his sudden loss of breath and scrambled back to his feet. A massive leg swept his own out from under him with incredible force. He flipped through the air in a near semicircle and landed on his face. Blood gushed out of his nose, followed by a numbing pain. His injured shoulder was in agony.

A sharp slice ran across his back. He cried out in pain and jolted up to his feet. Gripping the pool cue tightly with the heavy end up, he aimed at where he thought Hunter stood. He let it rip, torquing his body and swinging the cue with all of his might.

It stopped abruptly in mid-swing as if Hunter had caught it out of the air. It was yanked out of his hands and he stood dumbfounded in the darkness, forced to listen to the heartbreaking sound of the cue being snapped in half. Each piece of it clattered to the floor.

The enormous hand grabbed him around the throat again and lifted him into the air. Hunter slammed him into the wall and pressed his arm to his throat, pinning him to it. Mark's feet dangled helplessly in the air. Saliva sputtered out of his mouth as he gasped for air.

Hunter grabbed him by his injured shoulder and he screamed out at the pain of it. Hunter pulled his hand away, almost as if he'd been surprised by Mark's cry.

Then his hand returned a moment later, investigating his shoulder. As soon as he felt the wound, he dug his fingers into it, prying them around. Mark let out a sustained cry as he frantically clawed at Hunter's arm and tried to pull the hand away from his shoulder.

Hunter's fingers finally left the wound and were replaced by the unmistakable feeling of a large knife plunging into it. Mark screamed in perfect unison with Roger Daltrey blaring from the jukebox. He threw his hand up against Hunter's face, trying to push him away. The skin on his face felt disfigured, like a rough leather mask. He survived the blast from his house, but he was still standing on the porch when it happened; the fire must have melted his face. Despite Mark's protests, Hunter was unflinching.

The knife slid out of his shoulder and another scream left Mark's lips. He pushed Hunter's head away just far enough to squeeze a leg between the two of them, then he shoved off of his chest as hard as he could. Hunter stumbled into the opposite wall. Mark crumpled to the floor, his shoulder bursting with pain. He coughed repeatedly and tried to regain the breath that the killer squeezed out of him. His hands patted the floor for one of the broken pool cue pieces.

Hunter grabbed him by the ankle and yanked him across the floor. Mark landed on his chest and scrambled to get back to his feet. Just as he pulled himself up onto his knees, a large boot caught him square in the chest, sending him reeling backward. He sailed through the air and tumbled down a flight of stairs. His body came to a dead stop on an unforgiving cement floor, making him recoil and curl up from the numbing pain.

He was in the basement. He must have been. The hard floor under him was cold and dirty. As he started to drag himself across it, he heard Hunter's deliberately slow footsteps descending the stairs behind him. He had played with his prey for long enough and now it was time to finish it.

Mark weakly brought himself up to his feet and limped away through the darkness. Hunter was right on his heels and he had nowhere to go.

When Hunter reached the bottom of the stairs, he stood still for a while and looked in Mark's direction. He couldn't see him, but he knew Mark was there. He walked toward him, his gait slow and leisurely. He ran his fingers over the blade of his hunting knife, smearing them in Mark's blood. He played with it in his fingers, rubbing it back and forth between them as he slowly gained on Mark's beaten, limping figure. Just a foot away now, Hunter reached out and wrapped a thick hand around his throat from behind. He paused.

The two of them stood motionlessly for what seemed like a very long time. Finally, Hunter looked down and wrapped his hand around the broken pool cue that was stabbed into his stomach. His hand remained on it, as if trying to understand what it was.

Mark turned around and gripped the sharp piece of wood with both hands. He wrenched it upward and took a lunging step forward, shoving it farther into Hunter's body. A spluttering sound emitted from the killer's mouth and his knife clattered on the floor. Mark shoved it deeper still, and Hunter grabbed it with both hands, trying to pull it out, but he was beginning to lose strength. Mark gave it one final shove and Hunter fell to the ground. He writhed for a moment, and then he was dead.

Mark staggered through the darkness until he found a wall, then he went along it, looking for the breakers. He found a metal box and opened the cover, his fingers running inside along the familiar nubs of the switches. He flipped all of them and the lights in the basement came on.

Bright fluorescents lit up the space and highlighted Hunter's dead body in gruesome detail. His skin was completely burned and unrecognizable. A large pool of blood spread out around his body. The most horrifying detail was that his face was completely absent of emotion, as if he'd died in the most peaceful way possible. A chill shook Mark's body and he stepped past Hunter and climbed up the stairs.

He tried the doors in the lounge again, even shoving himself into them, but they wouldn't open. He pulled the fabric off one of the windows and used a barstool to shatter the glass and loosen the boards he and Felix had put up. A heavy gust of wind entered the lodge, followed by a torrent of rain splashing in his face. Mark stood on the stool and carefully climbed through the window.

He flopped onto the gravel path with a wet thud. He moaned and got to his feet. With the very last bit of strength he possessed, he headed for Hector's cottage—his only hope.

― CHAPTER TWENTY-FOUR ―

THE BLACK WARDEN RETURNS

Hector was in the kitchen tidying up. He paused and listened in disapproval at the harsh swell of the storm outside. He sighed and went back to washing his plate.

The front door burst open. At first he thought the storm had done it, and he put the plate down in the sink to investigate.

Mark was lying facedown on the floor.

"Christ Almighty!" Hector said and rushed over to him. He saw the wound in his shoulder, which was bleeding heavily, and made a disapproving noise. Mark was very pale and weak. Hector pulled him across the floor and helped prop him up in one of the armchairs in the living room.

"I'll be right back," he said, glancing worriedly at his wound. He turned and disappeared into the kitchen.

Mark's head rolled around on his shoulders, trying to understand his surroundings. His consciousness was quickly fading and his comprehension was starting to slip. There was a bottle of wine sitting on a small table beside his armchair. He grabbed it and yanked the cork out. It came out with surprising ease and he began chugging the bottle.

Hector came back out, holding a first aid kit. He moved to the other armchair and set the kit down, then he slowly approached Mark who was almost halfway through the bottle.

"Okay, okay," Hector said. "That's more than enough." He took the bottle away from Mark and set it down out of arm's reach. He pulled up the other armchair and took Mark's shirt off. Mark groaned as it went over his head, but settled down after it was off and his arms fell to his sides again. Hector went to work on his wound with the first aid kit in his lap. "All right... this *will* sting."

Mark winced as he started to clean the wound. After it was done, he fished through the first aid kit and took out a suture and some dressings. Sweat rolled down his forehead as he worked. He paused and took off his own shirt, revealing a sleeveless undershirt beneath. He lifted a large book off the table beside him and flicked through it, referencing it as he worked.

Mark flinched from the pain of the treatment, gasping to catch his breath between each poke and prod that Hector did. Once he managed to get his breathing under control, he began to tell Hector what happened.

"The book wasn't there!" he blurted. "And Nathaniel's body... it was *gone*." His chest heaved between sentences as he tried to catch his breath. "The thing... in the catacombs... it did this to me." His eyes rolled toward his shoulder. "And Hunter... he stabbed me, but... I killed him."

Hector raised his eyes and studied Mark for a moment, then went back to work.

"Felix is gone," Mark continued. "I think he might be dead... I think... it might be too late... Nathaniel is coming back..."

His eyes rolled wildly in their sockets, looking around the room. They brushed across Hector. He'd never seen Hector without a long-sleeved shirt on before. There was a large 'X'-shaped scar on the side of his left arm, just behind the bicep.

"Hector... I don't know what to do... you need to call the police..."

That 'X'-shaped scar. Where had he seen it before? It was so familiar to him, as if he'd read about it just recently.

He felt himself get weaker. Talking became very difficult.

"I think... somethin's gonna... happen... on that island... you... have to... go there..." Mark tipped his head and looked at the wound that Hector was tending to. "I think... you need... to call me... an ambulance..."

Hector stopped what he was doing and looked squarely into his eyes. "I don't think so," he said. His voice was colder than it usually was.

Mark blinked at him, not understanding. His eyes glanced again at the scar on Hector's arm. And then it came to him.

Nathaniel's body was missing from the sarcophagus because it was never there in the first place. The ritual book wasn't there because Nathaniel never parted with it. And Nathaniel couldn't be resurrected because he never died... because Hector *was* Nathaniel.

The memory came back to him. The 'X'-shaped scar on Nathaniel's arm... Nathaniel had mentioned in one of his journals that a worker had snuck up on him with a knife and cut his arm.

Mark swallowed in a hard gulp. The sight of Nathaniel sitting across from him was very sobering. Nathaniel looked at him with a dry smile then glanced down at the large book in his lap. It was the ritual book.

"But..." Mark started. "But..." An incredibly overpowering feeling washed over him, like he was about to pass out. He didn't understand why he felt like this. He looked around the room, trying to figure out what had happened to him, when his eyes stopped on the bottle of wine that he copiously drank. His eyes darted to Nathaniel and he opened his mouth to say something.

"Shh..." Nathaniel whispered. "You need to save your strength. I need you in tiptop shape." He leaned forward and clamped a hand on Mark's injured shoulder, then looked down at the ritual book. He began reciting foreign incantations as all senses drifted away from Mark and he was left with nothing but blackness.

— CHAPTER TWENTY-FIVE —

Losing Consciousness

Brilliant white blinded him. When his eyes adjusted to the change, he was able to see a set of bright lights above him, like what a surgeon would use during an operation. He tried to raise his arm to shield his eyes, but something held it in place. He twisted his head and saw that it was strapped to the table he was lying on. He tried to move his other limbs but they were strapped down, too.

He was in a small room. He had no idea where, but he could see a set of stairs at the end of it, leading up. It looked like a basement, but it was kept very clean and sterile. He slowly remembered what happened before he blacked out and realized he must have still been in Hector's cottage. No... Nathaniel's cottage. He blinked his eyes, hoping that it was all just a bad dream. His head was spinning, still woozy from the drugs in the wine.

"Good... you're awake."

Mark jerked his head to the side and saw Nathaniel standing by a long table pressed against the wall. His back was turned and he looked like he was fiddling with something.

"What do you want?" Mark asked.

Nathaniel turned and considered him for a moment, but didn't say anything. He didn't look anything like Hector. The man in front of him was cold and calculating, obviously not afraid of anything.

"Why me?" Mark pressed. "What do I have to do with *anything?*"

The same dry smile from before spread across Nathaniel's lips. "Mark, you were even more pliable than I ever hoped. Always so obsessed with 'saving your brother' and 'stopping Nathaniel's resurrection' that you started to forget why someone wanted you to come here in the first place. You know that old saying, what is it? 'Like a dog with a bone...'"

"And what's *your* bone?" Mark asked bitterly.

Nathaniel smiled and looked at something on the other side of Mark.

Mark turned his head and was greeted by the sight of a decomposed corpse lying on a table next to him. It was small, about the size of a young child.

"Is that..." Mark started.

"Your brother," Nathaniel said.

"Why?"

"That day, thirty years ago... it taught me something, you know." Nathaniel laughed. "Me, of all people, still learning after all these years." He turned and grabbed something from the long table. "That island can imbue people with unimaginable powers. At first I thought the presence on the island was merely destroying their minds, but it's nothing like that at all. They become like conduits for the presence. But none as much as your brother. He really is quite special. I hope you can appreciate that."

Mark said nothing. When Nathaniel turned his back again, he struggled against his restraints.

"I've never seen someone so sensitive to the island's presence," Nathaniel continued. "Even as a lingering spirit, he holds far greater power than anyone I've ever seen. The only problem is that he can't be controlled like the others. He's unruly. The true opposite of you. Where you danced like a marionette when I pulled the strings, Jamie shrugs them off. He can't be controlled; only directed. That's where you come in."

Mark snarled at him. "You can't make me do anything. You hear me? Not a damn thing!"

Nathaniel brought his face to Mark's. With a smooth, almost smoky voice he said, "You think you have a choice?"

Mark twisted his face in anger, but kept quiet.

"I thought so," Nathaniel said. "Who are you anyway, hmm? A consciousness inside a body? No, I don't need you at all, Mark."

"What are you trying to say?"

Nathaniel grinned. "Don't you get it? I don't need you, I just need your body. Your brother... oh, he never listens to me, but he listens to you, doesn't he? He trusts you? Once I install my consciousness into your body, he won't be able to tell the difference. I can use him to do exactly what I want; direct his immense power in whatever way I choose."

"What'll happen to me?" Mark asked quietly.

"For you it will be like floating in an unending limbo. You will be trapped in nothingness while your consciousness slowly degrades and goes insane."

A tear rolled down Mark's face.

"Don't feel too bad," Nathaniel said. "You'll be doing me a great service. After how long I've waited for an opportunity like this, I wouldn't be able to thank you enough."

"How are you still alive?" Mark asked.

"The presence has many great potentials. Think of it as the very essence of life. One such potential is to extend one's life and live forever. And that's what I'll be doing once your body is mine. To be honest, I've gotten tired of looking at this one in the mirror." Nathaniel leaned over and inspected Mark's shoulder. The wound was much smaller than before, some of the skin already turned to scar tissue, and any part that was still open was now stitched shut. "I didn't think you'd come to me in such rough shape, but apparently you're a bit of a slippery fish."

"Why did you send me down there?" Mark asked. "Why go through all the trouble?"

"Oh, it was no trouble," Nathaniel replied. "Believe me. I just needed an excuse to separate you and Felix. I took Pete and Jerry out of the equation in one fell swoop by subjecting Pete to a concentrated exposure to the island's presence. That also gave me the opportunity to see how you reacted to the presence when your mind was weak from alcohol when you went looking for him."

Mark thought of when he got in the boat to search for Pete on the lake and the strange layer of ashy dirt on the bottom of it. "That dirt was from the island..." he said.

Nathaniel nodded.

"It seems when your mind is weakened, even you're not immune from the effects. And so once it was just you and Felix left, I drew you away on a wild goose chase while I had Hunter take care of him. The Sentinel was supposed to bring you to me, and failing that, Hunter was to do the job. He played a little rough, but boys will be boys. I just wish I could have gotten you here sooner and spared the mayhem you caused, like killing Hunter and his brothers. They were like sons to me, those boys. I raised them, you know. Loved them like a father should. Three little boys vacationing at the lodge fifty years ago, plucked up by me. Why? Because I saw potential in them, too. Do you know that they even agreed to have their tongues cut out early on as a show of loyalty? Speak no evil..."

"You're sick."

"No. Not at all. You just don't understand what it's like to have this power at your fingertips."

"So this is the real you?" Mark asked. "None of that timid Hector afraid of the dark and afraid of the water?

That story you told me about the girl who drowned in the lake... that was just bullshit, wasn't it?"

"Partly. She was my daughter. I resurrected her from the dead in the cabin to experiment on her and she tried to escape. She made it all the way to the lake before I caught up to her and drowned her. Just a random Jane Doe. Of course the police believed it; she hadn't been alive since the late 1800s, so they had no record of her."

"Jesus Christ. Your own *daughter?*"

Nathaniel smiled. "It looks like we've both been responsible for the deaths of our families."

The words stung Mark, but he kept himself under control.

"So you really can resurrect someone?" he asked. "You weren't lying?"

"Of course you can. The process is detailed in this book, just like I said." Nathaniel gestured to the ritual book sitting on the long table. "But we're going to be using a different ritual today..."

The barrel of a shotgun gently pressed to Nathaniel's temple. Felix stood behind him, a toothpick sticking out of his teeth. He gestured toward a chair sitting against the wall. "Sit down."

A wave of relief washed over Mark.

"How did you find out?" Nathaniel asked.

"We found your little black book," Felix said. "There were transactions detailed between you and a lackey of yours named Hector Willoughby. Apparently Hector was a reclusive hermit who lived in this cottage until you killed him and stole his identity. Hector never went out in public, so no one knew the difference."

Nathaniel smiled. "I thought Firebug got that ledger in the fire. Nonetheless, very good."

"*Sit.*"

Nathaniel's smile faltered and he took a seat in the chair.

Felix fished a pair of handcuffs from his pocket and tossed them to him. "Put 'em on."

Nathaniel looked at the handcuffs for a moment then clamped them onto his wrists.

"I always knew there was something funny about you," Felix said. "When I figured it out, I drove into town to get the sheriff and found him murdered in his home. I tried going to the department, but all the officers were busy responding to calls all around town. Doing it during the storm was a smart play. After that, I realized that the place I should've been the whole time was right here."

Felix unfastened Mark's restraints, keeping his shotgun pointed at Nathaniel who sat patiently in the chair.

"Can you walk?" Felix asked Mark.

"Yeah," he said, and he slid off the table and onto his feet. The drugs Nathaniel slipped him still had a strong hold and his balance was shaky.

Felix waved the shotgun at Nathaniel. "Get up."

Nathaniel rose to his feet and looked at him with utter impatience. Felix motioned for him to head up the stairs and he turned and complied. Felix kept the barrel of the shotgun pointed at his back.

The three of them headed up the stairs and into the living room of Nathaniel's cottage. They went through the door that Mark had seen locked when he first visited. Nathaniel stopped and turned around, looking at Felix for further instructions.

"Out the door," Felix said, rocking his head toward the cottage's front door. "Come on, let's go."

Nathaniel gave him a smug grunt, then turned. As he took a step toward the door, it happened. Like a set of dominoes set into motion, Mark watched, powerless to stop it. Nathaniel tripped on the edge of a rug and stumbled into the wall. Felix stepped forward and reached out to steady him. Then Nathaniel planted his feet down and spun around. He threw his arms up and knocked the barrel of the shotgun away. It went off, blowing chunks of fabric out of one of the armchairs in a large puff. Nathaniel grabbed the barrel of the gun with both hands and yanked it, pulling Felix off balance and hyperextending his bad leg, then he stomped on his knee, shattering it and bending it the wrong way.

Felix screamed and fell to the ground. His grip on the shotgun loosened and Nathaniel took it away from him. The next second seemed to play out in slow motion. Felix tried to get up. Nathaniel aimed the gun at him and pulled the trigger. In the next instant, Felix was gone.

His body slumped on the floor. Something golden flew out of his breast pocket and tumbled along the rug. It was the T-rex locket he'd bought for his grandson's birthday party. The party he promised he would come to.

A HAUNTING AT HOLLOW'S COVE

Mark stared in disbelief at what happened. The strength left his legs and they began to wobble. He held onto the wall as he slid down it, mesmerized by the chaotic scene.

Nathaniel dropped the shotgun to the floor and walked over to Felix's body. He bent over and fished in his pockets, searching for the key to the handcuffs. While he was busy, Mark crawled across the floor toward the weapon. He lunged for it and spun around, pointing it at Nathaniel.

But Nathaniel was gone.

His voice echoed throughout the cottage, seeming to come from all places at once: "There you go again, Mark, thinking you can change things. Do you feel that insidious itch crawling through your head?"

The familiar tingling that Mark experienced on the lake invaded his brain. He tried to scratch it, but it was deep under his skin.

"Can you feel it warping and twisting your mind?" Nathaniel continued. "Can you feel yourself struggling against it while you're powerless to stop it?"

Mark gritted his teeth and furiously rubbed his palm against his head. He carefully backed into one of the darkened bedrooms off the living room and hid just beyond the doorway, holding the shotgun close to him.

The walls began to bleed. Thick red streams gushed down their lengths from the ceiling, staining and pooling on the floor.

The door to the basement slammed shut. It opened and slammed itself repeatedly, as if guided by an invisible hand. The noise of it increased in volume each time until Mark clutched his ears in pain. When he couldn't bear it anymore, the door slammed one last time then stopped. It slowly creaked open, revealing an opaque blackness behind it.

Jamie's blood-curdling scream came from the darkness, just as it had in the cabin. He walked out of the darkness a moment later and went across the living room to Mark. He looked up at him with a very sad look on his face. "Why didn't you help me?" he asked.

"I will!" Mark said. "*I will!*" Tears rolled down his face.

Tears rolled down Jamie's face, too. He extended his arms out and Mark did the same. When their hands were almost touching, another figure emerged from the blackened doorway.

It was their father, Bruce. He marched with the momentum of a freight train. His face was warped into a scowl as he barreled down on Jamie. Mark shouted in protest, but it was too late. Bruce grabbed Jamie by the head and snapped his neck in one rough jerk. His body fell to the floor and Bruce turned his attention to Mark.

"Why did you do this to me?!" he shouted. He grabbed Mark by the arm and yanked him forward. "WHY DID YOU MAKE ME DO THIS?!" He wiped his hand on Mark's bare chest, leaving a smeared, bloody handprint across his skin.

Mark wilted under the overbearing pressure from his father. "*I'm sorry! I'm so sorry!*"

Bruce turned around and started to run away toward the basement door.

"Wait!" Mark yelled as he followed his father.

Just as Bruce reached the end of the room, he sailed into the darkness. A noose caught his neck and he lifelessly swung back and forth. The rope twisted around. Bruce's eyes bulged out of his head. "*You did this to me*," he said in a strained gargle.

Then the basement door slammed shut, separating Mark from his father. He tried to open it, but the doorknob wouldn't even turn. He pounded on the door with his fist as tears streamed down his face. The itching in his head got worse.

"Daddy?" a soft voice from behind him said. He spun around.

It was his son, Jamie. He stood in front of Mark, tugging at his arm. Mark was speechless. On the floor behind his son were his wife and daughter just as he had found them that day. Jamie walked over and nestled himself next to them as if he were putting himself to sleep for the night.

Theresa sat up. Her face was cold and discontent. She pulled their children toward her like a protective mother bear. "Stay away from us," she said. "You've done enough."

Mark sank to his knees. "Baby, what are you saying? It's me, your husband!" He reached out toward Katelyn, but she shrank away from him. "It's your father! *Daddy!*"

The three of them backed away to the wall. Theresa suddenly screamed and a large splash of blood hit the wall behind them. As the dark red liquid dripped down the wall, it formed into the symbol of the Black Warden. Theresa, Jamie and Katelyn slumped over, dead.

"No!" Mark said. "*No! Please no...*" He bent forward and rested his head on the floor in front of them. "*Please no...*" he repeated in a low croak.

He suddenly felt a cold presence behind him. He turned his head and saw Nathaniel standing over his shoulder, dressed in a long black cloak. It was the same black cloak that he saw on his first night at the lodge— the mysterious person on the island.

Nathaniel extended his hands. "I can help you, Mark. I can save your family. Just give me your hand and I can help you."

Mark looked at his extended hands through thick tears for a long moment. He took one of them. But he kept his other hand on the shotgun as he got up to his feet. Nathaniel turned him around and directed him across the living room.

"Come with me, Mark. I'll help you. All you have to do is come with me."

"Okay," Mark said weakly as he shuffled his feet across the rug.

Nathaniel reached for the shotgun in his hand and softly said, "Give it to me, Mark."

Mark pulled the weapon away. "No, I'm gonna keep it," he said with the stubbornness of a child.

When they arrived in front of the basement door, Mark stopped. He stared down into the unending blackness. A cold chill seeped out from the depths and wrapped itself around him, making him shudder. The dreadful moan of the Sentinel bellowed from below.

His body clenched up. A voice in the back of his head screamed at him not to go down there. Just as Nathaniel placed a hand on his shoulder, he staggered away from the door and into the middle of the living room. He raised the shotgun and pointed it at Nathaniel. "No!"

Nathaniel raised his arms in defense. An apprehensive look spread across his face. "Don't get too hasty, Mark. You don't know what's real and what's not. You wouldn't want to hurt yourself..."

A noise came from behind Mark. He wheeled around and aimed the shotgun. It was Nathaniel, standing behind him now. He turned back to where Nathaniel originally was and found him still standing there too with a widening smile. He turned again and saw another Nathaniel standing between them. He kept spinning, frantically aiming the gun at each copy as they blossomed up all around him. Eventually, twelve of them surrounded him, each one smiling wickedly.

One of them lunged forward and reached for his shoulder. He swung around and shot at Nathaniel's approaching figure. The shot went right through him. He smiled, brushing his intact chest where the buckshot passed through.

"It's useless, Mark," he said in his omnipresent voice. "Give me the gun before you hurt yourself."

Another Nathaniel made a grab for him, but he pulled away. They taunted him as he wheeled around, his eyes like those of a startled doe.

He studied each one. One had his arms stretched above his head as if trying to scare him. Another was standing with his arms folded, looking smugly at him. One of them had his hands clasped together in front of his chest, as if in prayer.

Mark stopped. He was the only Nathaniel with his hands together. Not in prayer, but because he was wearing handcuffs.

He raised the shotgun and took aim at this Nathaniel. The smile quickly faded from all twelve of their faces.

Mark pulled the trigger. A red mist painted the wall behind Nathaniel as his body hit the floor. All of the others suddenly disappeared, as did the terrible itching in Mark's head. He stared at the dead body for a moment before dropping the shotgun. He grabbed his shirt that Nathaniel had taken off to patch him up and put it on.

The open door to the basement led down to a brightly-lit room. He stepped over Nathaniel and headed down the stairs. He paused and looked at his brother's decomposed body lying on the table. The corpse really was hideous, but Mark could only see him with love in his heart.

He grabbed a sheet of fabric draped over a workbench and wrapped Jamie's body in it. He picked up the ritual book from the long table sitting against the back wall and wrapped it in the sheet as well.

"*I will*," he said softly. He carried the body and the book back upstairs. Right as he was about to go out the door of the cottage, he stopped. He looked down at the floor and saw the golden T-rex that fell out of Felix's pocket. He picked it up, putting it in his own. "I'll make sure Jacob gets this. I promise."

He pulled the door open and once again braved the raging storm outside. He had one final stop to make, and then it would all be over. The place where it all started. The cabin.

— CHAPTER TWENTY-SIX —

THE CABIN

By the time Mark took a boat out of the boathouse, the storm had gotten even worse. He carefully set his brother's body down in the motorboat and set off for the island. Even in the distance, through all the rain and darkness, he could see it—a black silhouette standing at the back of the cove. He got the terrible feeling that it was waiting for him; beckoning him to come and join the ranks of the dead.

The woozy feeling he got from being drugged was still there, but fading. Regardless, he knew the island would still have an effect on him. He just had to move quickly. His legs felt weak, but he would run if he had to.

As the boat sped across the black, churning water, he hunkered over Jamie's body and the ritual book wrapped in the sheet, trying to shield them from the rain the best he could. Despite his efforts, tall waves crashed over the side of the boat and spilled inside from all directions as it bobbed and weaved through the rocky waters. There were several times when he gripped onto the sheet tightly because he was sure the boat was going to capsize. When he was about twenty yards from the shore, a large wave caught the boat and sent it reeling to the side. It rocked dangerously, on the brink of tipping over, but finally caught and crashed back down onto the water. He corrected the boat's direction and brought it in to shore as the overtaxed motor chugged and spluttered.

As soon as he stepped onto the island, he noticed that the wind and rain were gone. The land and lake all around the island were being severely battered by the weather, but it was totally calm where he was standing. He dragged the boat as far up the shore as possible and grabbed the sheet with his brother's body and the book in it. Just as he began to climb the hill, his head started to pound. The feeling escalated quickly and the invading itch joined it. When he got to the top, the itch was stronger than ever. He staggered forward and fell to his knees. Even though the drugs were starting to wear off, it seemed like the island's evil presence was somehow growing stronger. He breathed in rough spurts, trying to force the feelings from his head.

He glanced along the path leading down the hill and saw glowing wisps flitting in and out of the warped trees. He gazed upon them in horror. Their eyes were red, filled with an unmistakable bloodlust. They were all the people Nathaniel ever killed—all of them consumed by the island's presence.

Mark looked away in horror and rubbed his eyes. He rubbed them so hard that he thought he might poke right through them. With a great sense of dread, he slowly glanced at the trees again. There was nothing but the twisting, black branches and massive trunks jutting out of the ground—no eyes anywhere. He let out a cry that was a mix between relief and fright. He knew the feeling in his head would only get worse, and he needed to hurry.

He started down the hill, slowly and carefully. An image suddenly flashed in his mind, so vivid and powerful that he thought he was actually seeing it. It went by so quickly that it was impossible to tell exactly what it was depicting, but long enough that he knew it was something dreadful... unimaginable, even. He screamed at the shock of it and lost his footing. Tumbling down the hill, he slammed onto the flat ground at the bottom.

More images flashed through his mind in a rapid-fire succession. Gruesome acts were depicted, and he knew he was seeing the suffering wrought by Nathaniel's hands. His heart leapt at each image and his teeth clenched together. His muscles stiffened and he writhed around on the ground, trying to fight off the horrifying barrage. Right when he was on the brink of madness, the images stopped. He braced himself for the next one, but it didn't come. He sat up and opened the sheet to make sure the fall hadn't done any damage to Jamie's skeleton, and it was thankfully intact.

The itching in his head increased even more and he tried not to waste any more time. All he had to do was round the bend in the trail and get to the cabin. He got to his feet, cradling Jamie's body in his arms, and he rounded the bend. As soon as he did, he stopped.

A HAUNTING AT HOLLOW'S COVE

Where there should have been a cabin at the end of the trail, there was instead a long hallway, tiled along the floor and halfway up the walls with small, pea-green tiles. Dim blue lights were affixed in the ceiling over his head, bathing everything in a nauseating hue. A series of doors lined the hallway on both sides. It seemed like he was in a mental hospital. Mark felt a presence behind him and he gasped as he glanced over his shoulder. A pair of red eyes gleamed at him from a cloud of darkness. But instead of a spirit of the dead, they belonged to a large gargoyle-like creature. It had short, thick legs and long, spindly arms. Horns sprouted from its head. Its face was sunken into the darkness, but he could see the eyes and the teeth. It started chasing Mark and Mark ran. His bare feet slapped against the hard tile. The doors in the hallway started flapping open and slamming shut endlessly. Mark sprinted for his life. When he tired out, he desperately looked from door to door ahead for a place of refuge, but behind every one was another hideous gargoyle creature waiting for him with open hands and open jaws. Mark screamed and the sound echoed in a wave that faded into the distance ahead then came back from behind him and passed him in an endless loop. He squinted his eyes and peered into the distance, spotting the most terrifying detail of all: he could see himself from behind, mirroring every movement of his frantic flight; he was running in a loop, with no end and no escape possible.

"Nooo!" he screamed as he sank to his knees. And then he noticed the ashy dirt underneath him. He sprawled onto his back and saw the faint moonlight coming through the trees. He was out of that nightmare and back on the trail; the drugs were wearing off and his resolute immunity to the island's evil influence was being reconstituted.

The cabin lay ahead. The ghosts of the dead were lined up on each side of the trail leading to it. More moved through the trees all around. Mark got to his feet and hoisted Jamie's body into his arms. He took a step forward. The spirits watched him carefully, but they demonstrated no immediate aggression. He passed between the two lines, his soaking wet body chilled to the bone. He forced himself not to look at any of them, keeping his eyes only on the door of the cabin, like if he didn't look they couldn't hurt him. His arms tightened around Jamie like a mother protecting her baby.

Out of the corner of his eye, he saw the charred and glowing bodies of the three brothers next to him. Firebug and Cleaver were burned almost past the point of all recognition, and Hunter had the same melted skin and stab wounds to his torso that he had left him with. They gazed fiercely, but Mark ignored them, repeating over and over to himself that they couldn't hurt him.

The front door of the cabin opened, revealing pure darkness behind it. He remembered this view. He shuddered as the exact memory recreated itself. He had watched that door open thirty years ago and had seen his brother walk out from its black depths. The sight of the open door was just as frightening now as it was then.

Jamie's horrifying scream broke the silence and rang through the cold air. Mark's heart leapt and he peered closer at the cabin's doorway, expecting to see his brother. Just as soon as he realized the scream wasn't coming from the cabin, but somewhere much closer, he looked down at Jamie's body in his arms.

The sheet had come undone and Jamie's face was peeking out, looking just as he did thirty years ago, his eyes wide, screaming bloody murder. Mark dropped the body in terror and he instinctively jumped back from it.

He blinked and saw that Jamie's body on the ground was still the same inanimate, decomposed corpse that he had brought to the island; he hadn't come back to life and he hadn't screamed. Mark tried to calm himself, then he bent and picked up the body again, wrapping the sheet back over Jamie's face.

When he stood back up, Nathaniel was standing on the path in front of him. He wore the same black cloak as he did in the cottage. A devilish smile spread across his lips.

"Killing me changed nothing," he said.

Mark froze, shocked that Nathaniel's ghost actually spoke.

"This is just the beginning," he said. His smile grew wider and more crazed. "*This is just the beginning!*"

Mark closed his eyes and continued walking toward the cabin. Nathaniel kept repeating his last sentence over and over again, more maniacally each time. Mark refused the words. He made a promise to Jamie that he would help him, and he was going to see it through. Nathaniel had no power anymore; even if that wasn't true, Mark kept repeating it to himself to try to drown out Nathaniel's words.

Mark didn't stop walking. Nathaniel's voice grew louder and louder, and suddenly Mark's body was washed in an incredibly icy feeling. He trembled, but he didn't stop until he stumbled into the wooden steps leading up to the cabin's porch.

He opened his eyes and beheld the cabin in front of him, housing the very heart of the island's evil, unknowable presence. He walked up the steps, each one screeching under his weight. He stepped across the porch and wrapped his hand around the doorknob. It was as cold as ice, sending a chill through his body. He slowly turned it and pushed the door inward. The faint moonlight from outside crept into the cabin, but wasn't bright enough to reveal anything in the darkness other than the bottom of a chandelier and the edge of a wooden table with a lighter on it just inside the doorway.

Mark stepped into the cabin and rested Jamie's body on the table. He flicked on the lighter, which illuminated the space enough for him to see that the chandelier was filled with dusty white candles. He stretched onto his toes and lit them.

As if a gust of wind swept through the cabin, the lighter's flame was snuffed out and the door slammed shut. Somehow, the multitude of candles on the chandelier was only enough to barely light the interior of the small, single-room cabin, leaving many shadows.

Mark took a good look at Nathaniel's consecrated study. A long, elevated slab of stone took up the back of the cabin. It looked like an altar. It was stained with dark hues of red. The Black Warden's symbol was painted on the wall behind it with the same dark substance. A hand-crafted dagger rested on the edge of the altar. The wavy blade looked like it was crafted out of bone. Aside from that, the cabin housed a dirty throw rug, a tall wooden cabinet, a chair, and the long, heavy table that Mark set Jamie upon, covered in tools, stationery instruments, and reams of paper. But the most noticeable thing in the cabin by far was the deeply chilling feeling Mark got standing in there, both in temperature and in intuition. If his mind had been weaker, it might have shattered just like Jamie's.

When he got over the initial shock of finally being in the cabin—where it all began—he clumsily walked over to the table and opened up the sheet that covered Jamie's body and the ritual book. He pulled the book out, setting it down on the edge of the table and flipping through the pages, looking for the resurrection ritual. As each page turned, he felt undeniable fear course through his body. The book detailed other rituals and experiments that were so ghastly that he tried his best to keep his eyes off of them. Many of the pages contained a hand-sketched image of what Nathaniel was seemingly trying to achieve with each experiment. Some of the things in the book were very similar to what he'd seen deep down in the catacombs. His heart jumped when he saw a full illustration of the Sentinel. Detailed notes were scribbled beside it, describing the creature's desired anatomy. He saw notes and drawings describing what really resided at the bottom of the hole in the room filled with altars, and other things down there that he thankfully didn't stumble upon. He put a hand to his mouth in horror as he saw things in the book more terrifying still. A strong compulsion to just shut it rose up in him, but he stayed resolute, flipping each terrifying page with trembling fingers.

Finally, he found the passage. There was a quick sketch of the stone altar with the Black Warden's symbol behind it. Notes scrawled on the page to the side of the drawing jumped out at him. He eagerly read each instruction carefully. They were equally simple as they were frightening. The book described that in order to resurrect someone, the body of the person to be resurrected must be placed on the altar and then a large blood sacrifice must be donated to the body. The excitement quickly washed out of Mark as he slowly reread each word.

A large blood sacrifice.

A sudden fright shook him. He found it very hard to bring himself to start the ritual, but he knew it was the right thing to do. After all he had been through, there was a light at the end of the dark, twisted tunnel that ultimately led up to this moment. He was going to have a brother again. The thought struck him as strange, now that he was a grown man and his brother would still be a child, but that wouldn't stop him from loving Jamie with all of his heart. He would raise him as a son and in a way continue from where he left off as a father.

He looked at his brother's body resting on the table with a deep amount of love. As frightening as the place all around him was, knowing that he was going to see his brother again gave him all the confidence he needed. He lifted Jamie's body off of the sheet and carried him over to the stone altar. He gently rested him on it and took a step back.

A large blood sacrifice.

The words rang through his head again. He took a deep breath and glanced around the room. His eyes fell on the knife sitting on the edge of the altar. He picked it up.

He approached Jamie's body on the altar and raised the knife. His heart began to race. He lifted a trembling arm into the air and held his hand over Jamie. Mark laid the wavy blade of the knife against his palm and very slowly slid it across. He winced at the feeling, more bizarre than painful, and very quickly a stream of blood soaked his hand and fell through his fingers, dripping on Jamie's body. The deep red dripped and dripped, and Mark waited for something to happen.

But nothing happened. He became worried as his heart raced even faster. It *had* to work. Or was this just one of Nathaniel's tricks? The final hurrah as he found out all of his actions had been for nothing?

A large blood sacrifice.

The words ran through his head again. He understood the phrase just fine, but maybe he was a little too scared to accept the full meaning of it. He turned his arm over and looked at his wrist. His arm trembled even worse thinking about what he was about to do. He held the knife to his wrist, but he couldn't work up the nerve to do it.

Something cold touched his arm.

Mark jumped back in fright and saw that Jamie was standing next to him in his glowing, ghostly form. He rested his hand on Mark's arm. It was freezing cold, but somehow comforting. Jamie spoke no words, but his quiet stare was the reassurance Mark needed.

Before he could talk himself out of it, he slashed the blade of the knife along his wrist and turned the cut down toward Jamie's body below.

A thick crimson stream pulsed out of his wrist and splashed it. Several seconds passed and still nothing happened. His arm was shaking very badly now. He grabbed it with his other hand to steady it so he didn't waste any blood. The tremors went into his body and his teeth began chattering. He looked at Jamie's ghostly form next to him, but he didn't move, still just holding onto his arm and watching.

A minute passed without incident. Mark started to become really scared and he felt very weak and pale. Just as his nerves couldn't take it anymore and he was about to pull his arm away, it happened.

The flames in the chandelier flickered violently and the Black Warden's symbol on the wall behind the altar came to life. Its dry, darkened blood grew more vibrant until it was thick and wet again. The red symbol bled down the wall in fresh lines.

Jamie's ghost began to pull away from Mark. He wasn't moving; he was *being* moved. His form warped and swirled around his body on the altar until it was a streak of light. Not taking his eyes off of the spectacle, Mark backed up and grabbed the sheet from the table, then cut a long swath of the material with the knife. He dropped the knife and tied the fabric around his wrist, pulling it tight with his teeth.

On the altar, the light disappeared and Jamie's corpse began to twitch. His bony fingers stretched and moved around. His body subtly twisted around on the spot, like a newborn baby. Ligaments began to grow and connect to each of his bones. Tendons and muscles sprouted and attached themselves to his skeleton. Cartilage expanded as an intricate network of veins stretched across his body. Organs ballooned in his quickly-forming chest cavity and skin started to wrap itself around his body, stretching from head to toe. Hair protruded from his skin and grew to the length that it was when he died.

The restoration was finished. Jamie lay on the altar, looking exactly as he did thirty years ago. He coughed and opened his eyes, squinting and rolling his head on the stone to look around. When his eyes fell on his brother, Mark saw the recognition in them.

"Mark?" he asked in a soft voice.

"I'm here," Mark replied through tears. "I'm here."

Jamie began to cry and Mark grabbed the sheet from the table and wrapped his body in it. Mark gave him a moment, then Jamie wiped his own tears away and just said, "Thank you."

Mark pulled him in tight and squeezed him. He kissed the top of Jamie's head. Looking around, he knew their time here was done. Not wanting to waste another second and risk the island getting its hooks into Jamie again, Mark hoisted him into his arms and said, "We're going home."

Jamie just rested his head against Mark's shoulder. He looked exhausted.

Just before Mark opened the door, his eyes fell on the ritual book. Debating with himself for a moment, he picked it up and tucked it under his arm. Then he took a candle out of the chandelier and held the flame to the edge of the table. When it ignited, he dropped the candle and opened the door.

To his surprise, the path outside was empty. All the ghosts skulking around had disappeared, including Nathaniel. And it was hard to say for sure, but Mark felt like the island's presence had lifted, at least a little.

"We're going home," Mark reaffirmed, more to himself than Jamie. He hurried back to the boat as Jamie shivered, and when they were inside, Mark made sure he was secured for the rocky journey back.

A HAUNTING AT HOLLOW'S COVE

The storm raged bitterly as they got back on the water. The rolling waves rocked the boat, but not as badly as before. Mark looked over his shoulder and saw a glowing orange light somewhere in the dark silhouette of the island. But he wasn't satisfied yet.

He looked across the cove and judged that they were about in the middle of it. He took the ritual book and threw it overboard, watching it quickly disappear into the murky blackness.

And with that weight lifted off his chest and his little brother by his side, they left Hollow's Cove forever.

— CHAPTER TWENTY-SEVEN —

A New Start

Mark watched Jamie play with the other boys. He ran around the backyard, laughing and giggling, as he played a game of tag with them. Mark's mouth broke into a smile. He couldn't believe his eyes. What was once a distant and long-forgotten memory was now flesh and blood before him. It would take a long time before he would cope with the loss of his family, but seeing his brother just like he was all those years ago again, it gave him some small sense of peace.

"Your son looks happy," Stephanie said from the lawn chair next to him.

Mark looked over. "Hmm? Oh, yeah. I haven't seen him play like this for a long time."

"Why's that?" Stephanie asked.

Mark thought for a moment, trying to come up with the simplest cover rather than getting into the very long and seemingly tall tale. "He just hasn't really been himself for a while," Mark said. "He got his smile back, I guess."

Stephanie nodded warmly. "Well I'm glad he has some other boys to play with." She scanned her eyes across the yard, trying to discern her son from the flailing mass of young limbs. "Jacob!" she shouted.

Jacob's head perked up and he gazed at his mother from under a dog pile.

"Come over here!" she said.

Jacob excused himself by wiggling out from underneath the pile. He got to his feet and trotted across the grass.

"Jacob, I'd like you to meet Mr. Winters. He knew your grandfather."

"Just Mark is fine."

"Well don't be rude," Stephanie said. "Say hello!"

"Hello," the young boy said meekly. He stared at Mark as if he were waiting to be excused so he could go back and play.

"I'm sorry your grandpa couldn't make it today," Mark said. "I know he really would've wanted to be here. But I've got something he wanted to give you." Mark fished in his pocket and retrieved the golden T-rex locket Felix had bought. Mark held it by the chain, and Jacob stared at it, mesmerized.

"Cool!" he said. He grabbed it from Mark and turned it over in his hands.

"And what do we say?" Stephanie chimed in.

"Thank you," Jacob said absentmindedly as his fingers traced along the contours of the T-rex.

Mark leaned forward. "You can open it, just like this." He helped Jacob find the latch and pulled the dinosaur in half, showing him the small picture of a smiling Felix.

"That's my grandpa." Jacob said.

"It is," Mark replied with a smile.

"Thank you, Mr. Winters," Jacob said. Stephanie ran her hand roughly atop her son's head and Jacob gazed at the locket for a moment longer before setting it down and running back for the cluster of boys.

Mark glanced over at Stephanie and saw that she was tearing up. "He was a good man," he told her.

Stephanie nodded. She wiped the tears out of her eyes. "I know," she said. "We were exchanging mail for the past few months and I... I just regret not knowing him more. Not since I was a little girl."

"He loved you," Mark said. "No doubt about that. Jacob, too. You should have seen how he smiled when he talked about you two."

Stephanie's face lightened. She reached over and squeezed Mark's arm. "Thank you," she said. The two of them watched as Jamie zoomed by, being chased by one of Jacob's friends. "He looks like a real good kid. I know he's got a good daddy looking out for him, just like I did."

"Yeah." Mark didn't bother correcting her. From now on, in a lot of ways, Jamie would be his son, even though they were brothers. It would take a lot of getting used to, but Mark was willing to put in the work. And she was right: Jamie would have a great dad in him looking out for him. Mark smiled as he watched his brother play, his heart heavy from everything that had happened, but also hopeful of the future.

Stephanie lived on a big property and the backyard stretched past a big willow tree and down a hill to a creek. Jamie started to follow Jacob down the hill.

"Jamie!" Mark shouted.

Jamie stopped and turned.

"Careful, okay?"

Jamie watched him for a moment, then a smile came over his face. He nodded gleefully, then he turned and disappeared down the hill.

As the rest of the boys played within Mark and Stephanie's view, Jacob and Jamie came to the edge of the creek. Tall cattails stood up in the water. Beyond them and the thin creek was a small stretch of grass before the land broke into the woods.

"Come on, I'll show you something cool," Jacob told him.

"What?" Jamie asked.

Jacob leaned over the water and parted the cattails, then he jumped through them to the other side of the creek. He held them wide and allowed Jamie to jump through. Jamie giggled when he did, and Jacob motioned for him to come with him into the woods.

When they were surrounded by trees and the playful screams behind them were distant, Jamie stopped.

"What's wrong?" Jacob asked.

Jamie stared through the trees at something unseen. Jacob turned to look, squinting and leaning forward, but not seeing anything.

A stone sailed through the air and hit Jacob on the shoulder. The stone bounced and struck his neck before rebounding onto the forest floor.

"Ow!" Jacob cried, holding his hand to his neck. He looked at Jamie with stunned eyes. "What did you do that for?"

"He told me to," Jamie said.

"Who?"

"The man in the black," Jamie said, pointing.

Jacob looked again but didn't see anything.

"He's over there," Jamie urged. Jacob started to slowly walk off in the direction he indicated, intrigued. Jamie watched him go for a moment, then his eyes lowered to a small rock half-embedded into the forest floor. He bent and picked it up.

A familiar voice whispered something in his head. A wicked smile flashed across Jamie's face. His grip on the rock tightened, and he followed Jacob deeper into the woods.

If you enjoyed this novel, please consider leaving an honest review on Amazon. Reviews help me reach new readers and write great new books!

Want to be the first to know about a new release? Subscribe to Jeff DeGordick's newsletter:
www.jeffdegordick.com/subscribe

Or say hello on my Facebook and Twitter page:
www.facebook.com/jeffdegordickauthor
www.twitter.com/jeffdegordick

I'm always happy to hear from my readers! Send me an email at:
jeff@jeffdegordick.com

Other books by Jeff DeGordick:
The Haunting of Bloodmoon House
The Witch of Halloween House
The Winterlake Haunting
The Ghosts of Jasper Bayou

ABOUT THE AUTHOR

Jeff DeGordick is a horror novelist currently living in southern Ontario, Canada. Writing stories was his first passion as a child, but he's also had forays into testing and designing video games for a living, and a very brief career as a cook.

He began writing in 1994 at age seven, embarking on a long journey of spinning strange and scary tales, penning many short stories and partial novels as a hobby.

He is also the author of the Zombie Apocalypse Series and he's currently writing many more creepy tales!

Manufactured by Amazon.ca
Bolton, ON

14573847R00164